Iva Honeysuckle
DISCOVERS
the
WORLD

Iva Honeysuckle

DISCOVERS
the
WORLD

By Candice Ransom

Illustrated by Heather Ross

DISNEP · HYPERION BOOKS
New York

First Edition
10 9 8 7 6 5 4 3 2 1
G475-5664-5-12032
Printed in the United States of America

Library of Congress Cataloging-in-Publication Data

Ransom, Candice F. 1952–
  Iva Honeysuckle discovers the world / by Candice Ransom ; illustrations by
Heather Ross.—1st ed.
    p. cm.
  Summary: Eight-year-old Iva Honeycutt is determined to make her first great
discovery this summer—the treasure buried in her small town of Uncertain,
Virginia, that her great-grandfather sought for years—if only she can keep her
pesky cousin Heaven from interfering.
  ISBN-13: 978-1-4231-3173-1
  ISBN-10: 1-4231-3173-8
  [1. Explorers—Fiction. 2. Cousins—Fiction. 3. Family life—Virginia—Fiction.
4. Buried treasure—Fiction. 5. Virginia—Fiction.] I. Ross, Heather, ill. II. Title.
  PZ7.R1743Ivd 2012
  [Fic]—dc23   2011018248

Reinforced binding

Visit www.disneyhyperionbooks.com

SUSTAINABLE FORESTRY INITIATIVE
Certified Fiber Sourcing
www.sfiprogram.org

THIS LABEL APPLIES TO TEXT STOCK

Chapter One

The Shame of Iva's Third Grade Year

Iva Honeycutt was scolding her Cadet Blue crayon when Heaven's shadow fell across the porch.

"Did I tell you to stand next to Sea Green?" Iva said, not looking up. "You're supposed to be with the blues."

Heaven loomed over her. Her cousin was hard to ignore. She was a head taller and weighed fifteen pounds more than Iva. And she was a mouth breather. Heaven huffed wetly next to Iva's ear.

Iva shifted so she was sitting on the one thing she didn't want Heaven to see. The Shame of Her Third Grade Year.

Of course, Heaven saw. Her eyes were as sharp as a lizard's.

"I see a little corner. Is that your map?" she said. "You said you lost it."

Iva stuck the wayward Cadet Blue in the time-out row at the back of her sixty-four-crayon box, where crayons with peeled wrappers and broken tips were sent to think about why they were there.

"Did you fib to me? I'm going to tell Aunt Sissy." Heaven cut her eyes toward the door. She was the only cousin who didn't have the Honeycutt light brown eyes. Heaven's eyes were a shifty gray, like oysters in a mason jar.

Iva thought about sad little Cadet Blue. Maybe she'd been too hasty. She plucked the crayon from the time-out row and said, "Stand beside Cerulean and learn a few things."

Iva had spent all afternoon straightening out her crayons. On the first day of third grade, she'd marched into Miss Callahan's class with her brand-new box of sixty-four.

But Miss Callahan had a rule. No one could have more than twenty-four crayons, just like in second grade. Iva didn't think her teacher was very forward-thinking, as her great-grandfather Ludwell Honeycutt used to say.

She went home that day, picked her favorite colors from the box of sixty-four, and packed them into her old twenty-four-crayon box. All year the other kids asked Iva how she could have a Dandelion colored sun or a Robin's Egg Blue James River, when their suns were plain old Yellow and their James Rivers were dull old Blue.

Now school was over for the summer, and order was at last restored in Iva's crayon box.

"I'm talking to you." Heaven punched Iva in the arm.

"I hear you." Iva wiggled away, accidentally uncovering her map.

"You got an Incomplete!" Heaven shrieked,

spit flying. She always spit when she got excited.

"I did not!" Iva flipped the construction paper over.

"I saw it, Iva. *In-com-plete*. I got a B plus on mine."

Iva knew this. She knew every little thing about her almost-the-exact-same-age double-first cousin. Heaven lived right next door. Iva's bedroom window looked into Heaven's bedroom window. When Heaven sneezed, Iva reached for a Kleenex.

This year Iva had been able to escape from her cousin in school. Heaven had been assigned to Miss Park's third grade. Everyone in both third grades had had to make up continents, and their maps were displayed in the hall outside the two classrooms.

All but one.

"I'm telling Aunt Sissy," Heaven said again.

Iva stuck her little finger in the plastic sharpener in the side of her crayon box. She liked testing the limits of her power. The sharpener didn't even hurt.

"Mama knows I got an Incomplete." Iva hated that word. It made her feel half finished.

Her map had serious problems. Number one, she had *not* invented a continent, like they were supposed to. Why make up countries and rivers and mountains when there were so many real ones to discover?

Heaven had named her continent Cloudland, which Iva thought was stupid. Who could live on a cloud without falling through it?

Instead of making up a continent, Iva had drawn a map of the world. But she had made the United States too big. Russia, Japan, and China were scrunched along the far edge like squashed cockroaches. She had put Australia next to Hawaii, in the wrong ocean.

Iva didn't label half of the states. She had gotten bogged down in all those square ones. Kansas, Nebraska—who could keep them straight? And what about those states that began with *I*? The state discoverers should have come up with better names.

Heaven tapped a drawing on one corner of the map. "Lily Pearl?"

"Yeah." Iva had tried to erase her sister's drawing of a witch wearing a diamond tiara and spraying an arc of rays. The caption read, *Fancy Witch. Get You a Ghost* in Lily Pearl's scratchy kindergarten scrawl. Lily Pearl's masterpieces were always in ink.

"Howard doesn't dare touch my stuff," Heaven said, snorting through her left nostril. Once Iva had heard Aunt Sissy Two tell Iva's mother that Heaven must have adenoids the size of tennis balls. Iva figured an adenoid must be that little punching-bag thing she'd noticed in the back of her throat. Heaven must have two of them. She *would*.

"I'll make a new map," Iva said. "Better than this one. My honor is at stake."

Heaven kicked off her ladies'-sized pink flip-flops. "You still got the worst mark of anybody in the whole third grade."

"I don't care," Iva said, though she really did. "I'm a discoverer. Discoverers find places nobody has ever seen before."

Heaven pointed her big toe at the map. "Chicago isn't a state."

"It should be. Who ever heard of Illinois?" Yet this was the very thing that worried Iva.

How would she ever be a famous discoverer like George Washington or Admiral Byrd or her great-grandfather Ludwell Honeycutt if she didn't even know Chicago was a city? She was almost nine. She'd better get busy discovering.

With a black crayon, she scribbled her initials on one of the porch posts. "I bet Ludwell Honeycutt knew all the states *and* their capitals by first grade."

Heaven snorted through her right nostril. "Mama says our great-grandfather was a crackpot, who never paid his light bill. And he would drive a hundred miles an hour out of his driveway and then poke along on the wrong side of the road."

"He was *not* a crackpot!" Iva said. "Why are you here, anyway? Did you come over just to bug me?"

"You want to go with me to Cazy Sparkle's yard sale tomorrow? I'm looking to get me some embroidered pillow slips for my Hope Drawer. Special ones that say 'Good Morning' on one side and 'Good Night' on the other. That way I won't get bored making the bed."

Iva was bored just listening to Heaven. "Cazy Sparkle is a crook."

"She is not!"

"Then how come she has yard sales at weird times, like Tuesday morning and Thanksgiving?"

"Because she's looking for things to sell all those other days, that's why."

"You know where she gets that stuff?" Iva

said. "She sneaks into old people's houses in the middle of the night and steals their pot holders and tea towels. Then they come to her yard sales and buy their own tea towels back."

Heaven jumped up. "You never want to do anything I want to do!"

"You never want to do anything good, like discovering."

"You'll never be a discoverer," Heaven said, snorting through both nostrils. "You can't even pass geography."

"A fat lot you know!"

From inside Iva's house Mrs. Honeycutt said mildly, "Girls. Be nice, now."

Heaven aimed her tattling voice at the screen door. "Aunt Sissy, Iva won't come yard sale-ing with me tomorrow."

"I wouldn't go with her to the corner!" Iva called back.

"And she wrote all over the porch," Heaven threw in for good measure.

Iva stood up, grabbing her map and crayons. Once Heaven started telling on her, she wouldn't quit till Christmas. Iva stamped inside the house, slamming the door.

"I'll be here at eight," Heaven yelled after her.

"I'm not going!"

Heaven flip-flopped down the steps. "Eight *on the dot*. Don't be late."

Iva stormed down the hall.

Her mother was scrubbing Lily Pearl's latest creation, Party Witch, off the wall. "Did you and Heaven fall out again?" she asked.

"No. We never fell *in*." Iva thought that was funny.

Her mother didn't laugh. "Iva, Aunt Sissy Two and I always wanted to have our babies at the same time so you all would grow up best friends."

"Doesn't sound like much of a job to me."

Her mother was still talking. "Arden and Hunter. Lily Pearl and Howard. The others are best friends, but you and Heaven . . ."

"I can't help it, Mama. I don't like her, and that's that."

Iva went into her room, put her map and crayons on her desk, and flopped down on her bed by her tree.

She had asked for the tree for her fourth birthday. She remembered describing it with her hands—slender trunk, soft papery leaves. Her mother had said, "Iva, honey, wouldn't you rather have a baby doll? Or a teddy bear?" No, it had to be the tree or nothing. She got her fake tree, tall in its wicker pot, thick with silk leaves.

When she was a little kid, Iva had whispered her secrets to her tree. Now she clothespinned notes to the leaves. Slips of paper, scribbled with her hopes and dreams, places she longed to visit, people she liked and disliked.

Friends, neighbors, teachers, and especially relatives were either in favor or not, depending on how they'd treated her. The names of people she was mad at were clipped to leaves drooping at the bottom of the tree. The ones she liked earned spots on the top branches.

Most people rotated from the top to the bottom and back again. Except Heaven. She was assigned a permanent leaf at the very bottom, close to the floor. Her name-paper curled at the edges and was furry with dust.

Iva checked the bottom branches. Slips of paper were pinned to two leaves—Lily Pearl for messing up Iva's map, and Heaven in her usual spot. Iva moved Lily Pearl's name to the top of the tree.

That left Heaven all alone at the bottom. Which she deserved.

Iva made up her mind. This summer she would start on her life's ambition. And Heaven would *not* accompany Iva on her mission. Let her cousin arrange guest soaps in her Hope Drawer.

Iva Honeysuckle had a bunch of discovering to do. First on her list, finding the buried gold her great-grandfather Ludwell Honeycutt had spent his whole life looking for.

Chapter Two

Naked Witch and Johnny Cash

The next morning Iva sat up in bed with her pillow propped behind her back. Her dog, Sweetlips, dozed next to her, snoring lightly. She had named him after one of George Washington's foxhounds. Most people didn't know that George Washington was a discoverer before he became president.

Iva held a small black book with crumbling edges. *Weber Tire Company Record Book, Browning 8-8770* was printed on the front cover. At first Iva thought *Browning 8-8770* was a code. Then she figured out it was an old-fashioned phone number.

She touched the book reverently, as if it were

an artifact from King Tut's tomb. Earlier that year, Iva's father had cleaned out their attic. He came across some of his grandfather's belongings. He gave Iva her great-grandfather Ludwell Honeycutt's tire record book, a geography bee medal dated 1923, and a stack of old *National Geographic* magazines.

At night she leafed through the musty magazines, marveling at the black-and-white photographs of people living in foreign lands. One night as she was reading, two things fell out of the July 1949 issue.

The first was a letter from the secretary of the National Geographic Society in Washington, D.C. It was addressed to *Lowell Hunnicutt*. Iva had frowned at the misspelling of her great-grandfather's name. In the letter, the secretary told Ludwell he needed to actually *discover* something to be considered for membership.

Iva realized Ludwell must have written to the National Geographic Society, asking to belong.

She knew he never became a member of the Society.

But *she* would. She would carry out Ludwell's great dream.

Now she opened the cover of the black book. All the inside pages were labeled *Tire Pressure*. She picked up a mechanical pencil she had swiped from Arden. Iva believed mechanical pencils were reserved for geniuses, but why her older sister had one was a mystery.

On the first page, Iva crossed out *Tire Pressure* and printed *The Book of Great Discoveries Made by Iva Honeycutt*. She clicked the pencil against her teeth. Something didn't look right. She erased her last name and wrote something above it.

Now the heading read, *The Book of Great Discoveries Made by Iva Honeysuckle*. That was the name she'd called herself in first grade. When she made her great discoveries, she wouldn't have the same last name as Heaven Honeycutt. Nobody would guess they were even related.

Iva leaped out of bed and dressed in corduroy shorts and a T-shirt. The *National Geographic* magazine pictures always showed discoverers wearing shorts.

For her first great discovery, she could find the missing boundary line. Their town was called Uncertain because it was next to the invisible line that divided Hopewell County from Dinwiddie County. No one had ever figured out where the line

was. That would be an easy job for Iva.

But she had something much more important to discover.

She took the second special thing that had fallen from the *National Geographic* magazine and tucked it in her pocket, along with a packet of tinfoil.

As she opened her bedroom door, something pink streaked down the hall.

"Lily Pearl!" Iva hollered. "Better not let Mama catch you!"

"I'm Naked Witch!" Lily Pearl flashed past, a rhinestone bracelet spinning around her thin wrist, white-blond hair flying behind her like a bird.

Iva walked into the kitchen. Arden was slouched at the table, her alto sax in her lap. Arden's almost-exact-same-age cousin, Hunter, Heaven's older sister, sat across from her reading a Nancy Drew book. Hunter's summer project was to read every single Nancy Drew in order.

Iva's mother stood at the stove, flipping corn cakes. Lily Pearl zipped by, snatching a piece of bacon from the plate on the table.

"Lily Pearl!" Mrs. Honeycutt yelled. "Quit running in your naked strip and put some clothes on!"

"Can't! I'm Naked Witch!"

Iva slid into her chair and helped herself to a piece of bacon. "Can I have three corn cakes, Mama?"

Her mother looked at her. "*What* are you doing wearing corduroy when it's hotter than the inside of the devil's belly button? I'm having a heat stroke just looking at you."

"These are my discovery shorts. All discoverers wear shorts." Iva chewed her bacon thoughtfully. "Well, except Admiral Byrd. He would have froze to death at the South Pole if he had on shorts. Mama, I was reading one of Ludwell's *National Geographic* magazines last night. It was from October 1933!"

"Mama, you really ought to burn those moldy old things," Arden said.

Iva stuck her tongue out. "Anyway, I was reading about this place called Chosen." Iva pronounced it as it looked, "chosen." "It's called Korea now, but in the old days—"

Arden put the sax reed to her lips and blew. A wrenching sound came from it, like a rusty nail yanked from a board.

"Could you tell that was 'Ring of Fire'?" she asked.

"Oh, honey, I don't think you can play 'Ring of Fire' on a saxophone." Mrs. Honeycutt set a platter of corn cakes on the table.

Iva forked three of the crispy, brown-edged cakes onto her plate before Arden could beat her to it. Arden was a huge pain, but probably all twelve-year-old girls were.

This summer, Arden was in love with an old country-western singer, Johnny Cash. His songs wailed from her room night and day, and so did the screeching from her sax as she tried to play "I Walk the Line" and "Folsom Prison Blues."

"I need lessons," Arden said. "Somebody to teach me to play real good."

"Nobody in the world can do that," Iva said, slathering butter on her corn cakes.

"Do you hear anything?"Arden said to Hunter.

Hunter turned the page of her book. "Must be the wind."

Lily Pearl darted through again, her hair like the tail of a comet.

"Lily Pearl!" Mrs. Honeycutt yelled at Lily Pearl's naked back. "Is that my good rhinestone bracelet?"

"Mama, this place Chosen used to be the Land of Morning Calm. Isn't that pretty? And there's another place called the Hermit Kingdom—"

Arden's sax shrieked so loud, the lid of the sugar bowl jittered.

"Will you be quiet!" Iva shouted.

"No yelling," her mother said, then bellowed,

"Lily Pearl! Get dressed right this minute, missy!"

"—and people go to the Diamond Mountains and they find diamonds on the ground. They just pick them up." Iva glared at Arden, daring her to interrupt again.

"Listen to this," Hunter said. "'Carson Drew emptied the tumbler at one draught and fastened his eyes on Nathan Gombet.' What's a *draught*?"

"Mama, the Chosen ladies beat their clothes on rocks in the river. And then they club their clothes to make them smooth, on a sticklike thing. Mama, can we do that? Wash our clothes in the river? We could go down to Calfpasture Creek and—"

"No."

Iva gave up. Just flat out quit. She scraped her chair back and flung open the screen door, leaving two of her three corn cakes.

Nobody cared the least little bit that Iva Honeysuckle was off to be a great discoverer. All they cared about were naked witches and country-western singers. If she found a new pyramid, her family wouldn't even notice.

As she walked across the porch, Iva saw something that made her want to run back inside.

Heaven sat on the top porch step, praying. Unlike other people, Heaven prayed out loud any old time. In the market; on the playground at school; in front of the statue of the Uncertain Soldier. And now she was praying on Iva's porch.

"Do you have to do that here?" Iva said.

"I'm going to be a Sunday-school teacher. You have to be good at praying."

Iva couldn't believe that all Heaven aimed to be in life was a Sunday-school teacher.

With her face lifted toward the sky, Iva's cousin intoned, "Bless Mama and Daddy and Hunter and Howard and Arden and Lily Pearl and Aunt Sissy One and Uncle Sonny—" She paused to draw breath.

Iva thought Heaven was going to name her next, but instead Heaven said, "And can you make Daddy foreman at the box factory?"

Iva was a little peeved Heaven had left her off the list. "Why don't you ask for Uncle Buddy to be made *president* of the box factory?" she said. "That's a whole lot better."

"Daddy likes his job," Heaven said. "He just wants to be off the night shift so he can be home with me. And the other kids, too," she added, as if her sister and brother were nodding acquaintances.

Iva thought this was funny, considering Heaven had just finished blessing them all over the place. Her own father was away a lot, too. He was a long-distance trucker for traveling exhibits. Last summer he drove the Declaration of Independence clear to California. Now he was on the road with the Candy Unwrapped Sweet and Sour Taste show.

Heaven jumped up as if she'd been sitting on an anthill. "You're right on time. Let's go before everybody else gets Cazy Sparkle's good stuff."

"How do you know I'm on time?" Iva narrowed her eyes at Heaven.

"The sun is in the eight o'clock position in the sky." Heaven pointed to the sun, already hazy from the heat. "See? Eight o'clock on the dot."

Iva felt a prickle of irritation. *She* should know what time it was by the sun. That was the first thing a discoverer learned, in case they dropped their watch in a tar pit.

"Come *on*," Heaven said. She put her hands on her hips in that bossy way of hers.

Iva did *not* want her discovering plans messed up by Heaven. Since the day Iva was born, Heaven had bothered her like a rock in her shoe. This summer, things would be different.

"I forgot my money," she said. "I have to go back in."

"Hurry up, then."

Iva raced back in the house, slamming the screen door behind her.

"Iva, how many times—" her mother began, but Iva whizzed past.

She burst through the door of her room, startling Sweetlips. He thumped his tan-and-white tail, but Iva didn't stop to pet him.

She heaved the window open. As she climbed up on the sill, she thought, This is what real discoverers do! They jump off cliffs and out of jungle trees!

Her window was only two feet off the ground, but the thrill of adventure made her feel dangerously brave.

Without hesitation, Iva leaped. She landed in the hydrangea bush. Her mother wouldn't be happy about that, but Iva didn't care.

She ran across the backyard, delighted she had outsmarted Heaven. When she reached her father's shed, she stopped, sweating and breathless. She pulled the special something from her pocket and unfolded the creased yellow paper.

Ludwell's map.

Chapter Three

Euple Free

Iva tilted the paper away from the bright sun and squinted at the script. Some of the fine, loopy cursive had faded, but the handwriting matched the name inside the tire record book. Definitely Ludwell Honeycutt's.

Gen. Braddock. April 8 & 9, 1755. Wag__s stuck in red Virginia clay.

Stopped at __C-E-R-T___. Filled a brass cannon $30,000 g-ld. Buried 2 feet down, 50 paces east of a stre-m, where the ro-d runs North and South.

At the bottom of the paper was a sketchy map with arrows and squiggly lines. One of the squiggly lines was marked with a *C*.

The day after she found the map, she had taken it to school. While she was supposed to be doing math, she had filled in the missing letters. *Wagons. Gold. Stream. Road.*

The word printed in capitals had given her the most trouble. Was that an *N* or an *R*? What about the two blanks in front, and the three blanks at the end? Then she knew. *UNCERTAIN.*

Gold. Uncertain.

Ludwell Honeycutt had searched for buried treasure right here in town! And Great Discoverer Iva Honeysuckle was going to find it.

Now, as she tucked the paper in her pocket, something cold and wet pushed into the backs of her knees.

"Sweetlips!"

The dog wriggled from head to tail, a black, tan, and white blur.

"Okay, you can come with me. Maybe you can save me from quicksand."

Iva slipped into the shed. The shapes of the

lawn mower and her father's power saw squatted in the dim light. The shed smelled like cut grass and wood shavings.

She stared at the tools leaning against the wall. The shovel was taller than her head. No good. The ax looked cool, but she couldn't dig with it. Then she spied a small tool with one blunt end and one sharp end. A pick.

She hefted it with both hands. Kind of heavy, but she could handle it. She swung the pick over her shoulder and set off on her mission with her trusty dog.

"Guess what I found out?" she said as they walked down Quarry Street. Sweetlips gazed up at her in fascination.

"Back in the olden days, this British guy General Braddock came to America with his army."

Sweetlips nipped a flea on his back. He scratched so furiously, his legs slid out from under him, and he fell over.

She frowned at this untrusty-dog behavior. "General Braddock had to go to Pennsylvania to fight the French because they wouldn't behave. He started in Virginia, but there was no road. So he chopped one through the wilderness. But he brought too much stuff and had to dump some of it."

Sweetlips attacked the flea again, digging until both ears flipped inside out.

"General Braddock finally got to Pennsylvania, but he was killed in the battle."

When Iva had read all this in the library, Ludwell's note became clear as glass. General Braddock had brought his war chest—gold to pay his soldiers. He buried the heavy gold in a cannon so he wouldn't be stuck in the red Virginia clay and could go on to Pennsylvania.

"Here's the best part," Iva said. "He buried the treasure *right here in Uncertain,* and I'm going to find it. I'll be famous. If you're good, you can have a gold coin."

They had reached Quiet Hours Avenue. Iva wished she lived on this street. There were no quiet hours in her house, or even quiet minutes.

On the corner sat a house like one of Mrs. Priddy's bride's cakes. It was tall and white, with curlicues and a big porch swooping all the way around the house.

Walser Compton was in her garden, mulching her peonies. Miz Compton believed flowers were

like people. Once, she told Iva that her feathery peonies looked like ladies that had been out dancing all night.

"Hey, Miz Compton!" Iva called.

Walser Compton straightened up and shaded her eyes against the sun.

"Where are you off to, Miss Iva Honeycutt?" she asked.

Iva wished she could tell her. Miz Compton was really neat. Once, when Iva asked her how old she was, Miz Compton replied, "My age is an unlisted number."

Miz Compton let Iva pick bachelor's buttons in her garden and sit by the goldfish pond. Sometimes they shared unsweetened cherry Kool-Aid and preacher cookies on the big porch. Iva considered Miz Compton her best friend.

"Got something important to do," she said.

Miz Compton nodded but didn't bore Iva with any grown-up stuff, like "Don't get chiggers," or "Stay away from the trash dump."

Instead she said, "Stop by if you want, and tell me your adventures."

"I will," Iva said. Miz Compton was always interested in her discoveries. Iva would surprise her with her great discovery and give Miz Compton a gold coin, too.

The hot sun was directly overhead. Iva felt her arms turn pink. Quiet Hours Avenue narrowed into a lane bordered with Queen Anne's lace and blue-flowered chickory.

She stopped at an outbuilding made of plain gray boards. A Tom's Peanuts sign hung crookedly over the doorway. Old hubcaps leaned against one wall, and a steering wheel was draped over a low branch of a maple tree.

A long-haired man wearing a shirt with *Central Garage* stitched on the pocket was shaping a piece of tinfoil over the fender of an old pickup truck.

"Hey, Euple," Iva said.

Euple Free looked up. His broad, tanned face

split into a grin, revealing a chipped front tooth
that Iva had always admired.

"Hey, yourself," he said. "How's the old pup?"
Sweetlips flung himself on the ground so Euple
could tickle his stomach.

Iva propped the pick against the bumper of
The Truck and took the packet of tinfoil from
her pocket. "Brought you some gum wrappers."

"Great. Thanks." He added her wrappers to
a stack of foil on the roof of the pickup. "The
Truck says thanks, too."

Iva noted Euple's progress. He was covering his entire truck with tinfoil. So far, only the hood and one fender were silver. The rest of The Truck was patchy with rust.

"Want to help?" he asked her. He handed her a Popsicle stick.

"Yeah." Iva placed the foil on the fender and rubbed the Popsicle stick over it. "You've been working on this forever. How come it's taking so long?"

"I like watching The Truck get all shiny a little at a time. I guess I like doing it better than I want to see it done."

Iva thought about this. If she was making something, she wanted to finish as quick as possible. Her mother claimed she had the patience of a newborn gnat.

"Have you raced The Truck lately?" she asked.

Euple smoothed the foil over the fender. "Nope. My truck is still the third-fastest pickup in Uncertain."

This was something else Iva didn't understand. The summer before, there was a big pickup truck race on Hopewell Road. Miz Compton's nephew Peter, editor of *The Uncertain Star*, came in second. Swannanoah Priddy won first prize.

"How come you don't race Peter Compton and Swannanoah Priddy again?" Iva asked. "I bet you could beat them this time."

Euple gazed up at the sky. "You know, I thought on being the second fastest, but then I'd worry about trying to be first, and that would cause me undue anxiety. I like being third. It gives me space to dream about being number one."

Iva stared at him. She had never heard anything so ridiculous. Who wouldn't want to be in first place?

Remembering her mission, she changed the subject.

"Euple, I'm looking for a road that goes north and south by a stream. Do you know what road that is?"

"Plank Road runs north and south," he said. "Every day, The Truck and me drive to Central Garage. The sun comes up on the passenger side when we go through Dawn. That's east."

Dawn and Central Garage, which was really just a garage, were the two towns closest to Uncertain. Calfpasture Creek ran alongside Plank Road.

Calfpasture Creek must be the wiggly line marked *C* on Ludwell's map, Iva decided. All she had to do was walk fifty paces east somewhere along the creek and wind up near the road. Easy peasy.

"Gotta go," she said, hefting her pick over her shoulder. "Come on, Sweetlips."

The dog was napping under a maple tree. Sweetlips slept twenty-three out of twenty-four hours.

They cut across the field to Plank Road. Calfpasture Creek muttered nearby. The sun had moved a little, but Iva still didn't know where east was.

"Sweetlips," she said sternly, "you're a hunting dog. Show me where east is."

Sweetlips was really just a mutt, but Iva knew discoverers often had smart hunting dogs on their expeditions.

He flopped on the ground and thumped his tail.

Iva took that as a sign. She marched in a direct line from the dog's tail to the creek. Then she stopped. The map didn't tell her where to start walking.

One place was as good as another, she thought, counting her steps away from the creek. She lost track between twenty-nine and thirty paces because she tripped over a rock and had to start over.

When she was exactly fifty paces from the stream, she grasped the pick by the end of the handle and swung it over her head. And toppled over backward.

She lay there, her breath knocked from her, and noted that her faithful dog was gazing longingly at a butterfly. "Thanks a lot," she said, stumbling to her feet.

This time she gripped the handle tighter and heaved the pick into a tuft of grass. Cement was softer! The pick bit into the ground about half an inch. She chipped away until her arms felt like rubber. Being a discoverer, she realized, was *not* easy peasy.

The sun beat down mercilessly. She needed a pith helmet, but would anyone buy her one? No-o-o. Her family wouldn't care if her brains fried.

She staggered down to the creek to splash water on her face. As she bent over, Sweetlips bounded between her legs in hot pursuit of the butterfly. Iva fell in the mud.

"You! Dog!" she sputtered in disgust. Now her front was as dirty as her back.

She struggled up the bank to dig some more. After a few more swings, she quit. Her palms were red. Her T-shirt and corduroy shorts were grubby, and her dirt-clogged socks scratched her ankles. For all that work, she had dug a hole only three inches deep.

She thought about Euple Free patiently covering his truck with tinfoil. He wouldn't have given up as fast as she did.

"Maybe this isn't the right spot," she said to Sweetlips. "We'll try again tomorrow someplace else." She left her father's pick lying in the weeds.

Iva thought she would never make it home. She was sweaty and tired and thirsty. She imagined being lost in the Sahara Desert, half crazed with thirst.

When she reached the front gate of her house, she got down on her hands and knees and started to crawl toward it. She hoped her mother would see her clawing up the sidewalk, tongue hanging out.

She pictured the scene. Her mother would rush out. She would carry Iva into the living room and settle her on the good sofa that only company was allowed to sit on.

She'd make Arden fetch ice water, and tell Lily Pearl to get extra pillows—

Iva looked up.

Heaven was perched on the top porch step, picture-perfect in crisp white shorts and a clean white T-shirt. A basket sat on her lap.

She smiled at Iva.

Chapter Four

Yard Sale

Iva stood up, brushing grit from her palms and knees.

"You're all dirty." Heaven flicked a speck of lint from her spotless shorts.

"I've been working. Unlike some people," Iva said.

Patting back a fake yawn, Heaven said, "You should have come with me to the yard sale. Want to see what I got?"

Iva collapsed on the steps. "A basket. Big deal."

"It's not the basket," Heaven said archly. "It's what's *in* it." The basket jiggled slightly.

Iva sat up.

Heaven reached in and lifted out a black,

brown, and orange kitten. Half of its nose was splotched brown and the other half, orange. A patch of orange fur bristled on the kitten's forehead as if it had been sewn on at the last minute.

The kitten stared at Iva with round orange eyes. Iva had never seen a cat with orange eyes before.

Wiggling all over with delight, Sweetlips pushed between Iva and Heaven, and snuffled the kitten. Indignant, the kitten batted Sweetlips's nose.

"You bought a kitten at Cazy Sparkle's yard sale?" Iva asked.

"For fifty cents," Heaven said, as if

she had scored the deal of the century. "I couldn't find any embroidered pillow slips to save my life—"

"You bought a kitten at a yard sale?" Iva could not believe her cousin's luck.

Heaven kissed the kitten's orange patch. It mewed in protest. "Isn't she the cutest thing? I named her Yard Sale."

This was too much for Iva. She'd slaved in the blazing sun all day trying to find Ludwell's treasure. All she had for her trouble were blisters. Heaven had strolled over to Cazy Sparkle's sleazy yard sale and come home with a fluffy little kitten. It wasn't fair.

Iva ached to cuddle the kitten. "Can I hold her?"

Heaven swooped Yard Sale away. "No. She's mine."

"Does Aunt Sissy Two know you got her?" Iva asked, suddenly feeling mean. "She'll make Howard sneeze."

Heaven's younger brother, Howard, was allergic to everything but rocks. Even Sweetlips wasn't allowed in Heaven's house.

"Mama won't mind." But Heaven's confident tone was edged with doubt. "I'll keep her in my room."

"Aunt Sissy Two will make you get rid of her. You'll have to give her away." Iva was enjoying this. For once, she got to needle Heaven, who drooped like an unwatered plant. "I'm sure Yard Sale will go to a nice home."

"I won't give her back!" Heaven clutched the kitten to her chest. "And you better not tell on me!"

Iva made her eyes big and innocent. "Me? Tell on you?"

Heaven looked at her warily. "You're just jealous because my kitten is cuter than your old Sweetlips."

There was some truth to this. Sweetlips was a good dog but kind of dull. Yard Sale was tiny and bright-eyed and playful.

"If Aunt Sissy Two says you have to get rid of Yard Sale, I'll take her," Iva offered generously.

"You will *not* get my kitten," Heaven stated. "And you *will* go to vacation church school."

"What?" Iva stiffened.

"I saw Miz Compton at the yard sale. She was looking to buy a tea ball," Heaven nattered on. "She ran over her old one, and now it's flat as a gander's foot—"

"Get to the church school part!" Heaven always dragged out her stories to infuriate Iva.

"Miz Compton told me vacation church school starts Thursday. She's the teacher, you know."

Of course Iva knew Walser Compton taught Sunday school at the Joyful Noise Temple of Deliverance Church. And that she taught vacation church school every summer.

"What else did you talk about?" Iva hoped Miz Compton had bragged how smart Iva was, being a discoverer and all.

"Miz Compton gave me a quarter so I could buy Yard Sale," Heaven said. "I only had twenty-five cents."

Iva blinked. Miz Compton was *her* friend.

"*And* she made me her assistant at church school." Heaven snorted from her left nostril, her bossy self back. "I'm in charge of the flannel board. Maybe I'll make you *my* assistant."

Iva would rather crawl in a hole and pull it over her than be Heaven's assistant.

"I don't have time for church school. I have work to do."

Heaven scooped up Yard Sale, who was stalking Sweetlips. Sweetlips quivered with bliss.

"I already told Aunt Sissy One. You have to go."

Iva's mother and Heaven's mother were sisters. They called each other Sissy. Iva's mother was Sissy or sometimes Sissy One. Heaven's mother was Sissy Two. They married the Honeycutt brothers, Sonny and Buddy, which meant Heaven was Iva's double-first cousin. Their mothers did everything together and felt their children should too.

Iva was tired of being thrown on top of Heaven like they were survivors in a train wreck.

She heard the sound of her mother running water in the sink.

"Mama!" she yelled through the screen door. "I am *not* going to church school!"

"Yes, you are," her mother said in her "that's that" tone.

Iva glared at Heaven.

Heaven's oyster-colored eyes glittered in triumph. "Told you." She grinned like a possum in a persimmon tree.

The four o'clocks had opened their trumpet-shaped blooms on either side of Miz Compton's gate. The flowers only blossomed in the late afternoon.

As Iva unlatched the gate, she wondered if she

could use four o'clocks to tell time. That would beat Heaven and her dumb old sun.

Walser Compton sat in her rocking chair on the porch. A sweating pitcher of cherry Kool-Aid and a platter of preacher cookies waited on the wicker side table.

"I thought you'd be by," she said.

Iva flopped in the other rocking chair, nearly launching herself backward. "It's been a rough day."

"I can see that." Miz Compton poured Kool-Aid into a jelly glass ringed with pink elephants. It was Iva's favorite glass, even though she was too old to drink from it.

She sipped tart Kool-Aid, then reached for a preacher cookie. "Did you make these because you could see me coming?"

Miz Compton laughed. "You're sharp as a tack, Iva Honeycutt."

Once Iva had asked why the chocolate oatmeal cookies had such a weird name. Miz Compton

told her that back when her father was a pastor, he traveled to several churches to preach the sermon.

"After church, farm wives could see Pa driving over the hill in his rickety car," she had said. "They'd whip up a batch of these cookies, because you don't need to bake them."

Now she asked, "Want to tell me what happened today?"

"No. Yes." Iva decided to leave out her failed treasure hunt and start with the bothersome part.

"How come you helped Heaven buy that kitten? And how come you made her your assistant at church school? Why not me?"

"Let's go back to front, shall we?" Miz Compton said. "First, you have never—um, *flourished* in vacation church school." She spoke as if Iva were one of her delicate orchids. "And I didn't think you would care to be my assistant."

"I might. But you never asked."

Miz Compton nodded once. "I should have

taken your feelings into consideration. But Heaven begged me—"

"That's not the way she told it! She made it sound like you crowned her queen or something." Iva's voice rose in a fluting imitation of her cousin. "'I'm in charge of the flannel board.'"

"Heaven does do a fine job setting up the Pharisees scene," Miz Compton said. "Now, about the kitten—"

Iva sat up so fast, Kool-Aid sloshed out of her glass. "You helped her buy it! I bet you wouldn't buy me anything *I* wanted."

"Iva, Iva. You don't need anything. You're . . . self-sufficient."

"Really? You mean, like a discoverer?" Iva forgave Miz Compton a tiny bit, like opening a door a slit.

"Exactly. But Heaven doesn't have your ability to make her way in this world."

"Yes, she does. She's bossy and she tattles

on me for every little thing. Heaven *always* gets her way."

Miz Compton sighed. "I admit Heaven could steal the joy from a snow day in Florida. But I think she's insecure. Maybe even a little afraid."

Iva wasn't swallowing this. "Afraid? Heaven? Is that why you helped her buy Yard Sale? Because you felt sorry for the big fat phony?"

"Partly. But mainly because Heaven seems lonely. She needs a friend." Miz Compton looked pointedly at Iva.

Iva crossed her arms over her chest. "It's not my fault nobody likes Heaven. She's sneaky, and she gets people in trouble. I will *not* be her friend. And that's that."

Her mother's words were good enough for her.

Miz Compton began gathering up the glasses and pitcher. "I'll see you Thursday," she said.

Iva rocked angrily, making the chair judder across the floorboards. "I'm only going because Mama is making me!"

"Yes, I know." Juggling the tray, Miz Compton pulled the front door open.

Iva got up and held the door, finally remembering her manners. "Thanks for the Kool-Aid and cookies."

Miz Compton smiled. "Why don't you go sit by the goldfish pond? You like to do that."

"Thanks. I will."

Iva walked down the gravel path around to the backyard. The goldfish pond had been built by Mr. Compton, who had died long before Iva was born.

She lay on her stomach on the cool flagstones. Below, huge fan-tailed fish swam slow and deep beneath the lily pads.

Iva gazed into the pool, trying to see her future. Would she be a great discoverer? Would she find the buried treasure? A new thought niggled free. Would Miz Compton be her best friend forever?

But she saw only dark, murky water.

Chapter Five

"Dozing" for Gold

Every Wednesday morning, Iva arranged the objects on her dresser. Her "earthly belongings." She'd gotten the term from her great-grandfather.

Ludwell Honeycutt had written a last will and testament. He didn't have any money, but he'd left his "earthly belongings" to his relatives: his favorite pipe, a white shirt with frayed cuffs, and the trunk full of stuff no one wanted. Iva had gotten some of the things from that trunk.

Iva placed Ludwell's lucky silver dollar in its spot of honor in the center of her dresser. She fanned blue-jay feathers like a crown above the coin. Sparkly rocks from Calfpasture Creek flanked the design. Iva nudged one rock that had slipped out of position.

Sweetlips was standing on his hind legs at the window. His doggy breath fogged the glass.

"What is it?" Iva looked out the window at Heaven's house next door.

Yard Sale teetered on the windowsill of Heaven's bedroom window. Her little red mouth opened like a baby bird's in a silent mew. Sweetlips howled.

A large body appeared at the window. Heaven picked up Yard Sale. She saw Iva watching and waved cheerfully. Then she pulled the shade down.

"She has that cat in her room!" Iva said to Sweetlips. "I bet she's hiding her!"

She yanked her own shade down, angry. Heaven not only had an adorable kitten, but now she had a secret, too. A secret almost as good as Ludwell's treasure.

Thinking about her great-grandfather, Iva

went into the kitchen. Her mother sat at the table, copying a poem from her latest chain letter.

"Mama," Iva said. "What was Ludwell Honeycutt really like?"

Her mother laid her pen down. "I didn't really know your great-grandfather. He passed before I was born. But your daddy was little when Mr. Honeycutt was alive. He said his grandfather would reach into his pocket and give him a butter rum Life Saver. Mr. Honeycutt always carried a roll."

"That's it?" Iva said, disappointed. She had hoped Ludwell had had a mysterious past. "Heaven said he was crazy. She's making that up, isn't she?"

"Arden thinks I'm crazy because I answer chain letters," her mother said. "I can't break the chain or we'll have bad luck. So I copy the letters to ten friends and send them off. You never know."

Her mother sent the letters to the same ten people, who were probably tired of having to send ten letters to *their* friends.

"What's that got to do with Ludwell?" Iva asked. Nobody in her family ever stayed on the subject.

Her mother didn't answer right away. Iva waited. At last she said, "Ludwell was turned funny. He was—different. Not bad-different. Interesting-different."

Interesting-different. Iva liked that. *She* was interesting-different too.

"Iva, honey, scoot down to the post office and get me some stamps." Her mother took a five dollar bill from under the sugar bowl and handed it to Iva. "Bring back the change."

"Okay."

Iva slammed out the door, Sweetlips on her heels. She raced downtown as if she were running to a fire. At the Uncertain post office, she bought ten stamps.

Outside again, she paused in front of the shop next to the post office.

"Are you feeling peaked?" Iva said to Sweetlips. "Me, too."

She walked into Priddy's Taxidermy and Cake Decorating. Sweetlips flopped just inside the entrance as if he would never move again.

The store was divided by a blue line painted on the floor. On one side, Mrs. Priddy ran her cake decorating business. *Wedding Cakes a Specialty*. Cubed samples of cupcakes were often offered on a china plate. Mrs. Priddy's half was neat and clean.

The sign on Mr. Priddy's counter said, ~~Taxidermy~~ *Just Plain Taxes*. His side was not so tidy. Stubs of pencils, stacks of paper, and a battered dictionary covered his counter. His single stuffed specimen—a gloomy-looking turkey vulture named Deadeye—hunched over the counter on a wooden perch.

Iva thought dead stuffed animals were creepy, but once she had asked Mr. Priddy why he didn't have any others besides the dusty buzzard.

"The taxidermy business isn't what it used to be," Mr. Priddy had answered, looking as gloomy as the vulture. "People today are offended by hunting and stuffing animals. That's why I've switched to income-tax preparation."

Iva headed for Mrs. Priddy's side of the store first. The china plate was as clean as Sweetlips's dish after Iva fed him his favorite leftovers, liver and onions.

"No cupcakes?" Iva had her mouth set on a taste of Sunshine Cupcakes.

Mrs. Priddy wiped her hands on her apron. A puff of flour flew up. "Sorry, Iva. I'm busy with a bride's cake for the Henderson girl. Her shower is Saturday."

Iva glanced at a white-iced cake in the display case. Blue and green frosting swirled around the seven layers. Tiny silver balls dotted the top. The cake had been sitting in the case as long as Iva could remember.

Mrs. Priddy followed Iva's gaze. "Swannanoah's

bride's cake. The first one I ever baked with my grandma's recipe. She was engaged to Donald Slout. Swannanoah, not my grandma."

Iva listlessly picked at a scab on her elbow. She'd heard this story before.

"But she got cold feet and hopped into that pickup truck of hers and hightailed it to the border."

Iva pictured Swannanoah with snow-covered feet, zooming down Main Street.

Mrs. Priddy dabbed her eye with the corner of her apron, leaving a floury smudge on her cheek. "'Course, she only drove to the county line, but still. She broke that boy's heart. And mine. There is nothing like a mother's heartbreak over her daughter."

She peered at Iva over her glasses, as if Iva might be aiming to do the same to her mother. Iva never thought about getting engaged. She didn't even like boys much.

"Swannanoah missed the boat," Mr. Priddy remarked from his side of the shop. "Donald Slout runs his own appliance repair shop over to Dawn. Even if he did drive his car to sixth grade."

"How old *was* he?" Iva asked, wondering if she could drive to fourth grade come September. She pictured Sweetlips riding beside her.

"Maybe not to sixth grade, but he was left back quite a few times. Swannanoah couldn't have done better. That shop of Donald's is a big concern."

"What's wrong with it?" Iva asked.

"'Concern' also means a business," Mr. Priddy replied.

He scratched his jaw with his pencil. Except during tax season, Mr. Priddy spent his days working crossword puzzles. Iva admired the big words he knew.

"Iva, tell Mr. Priddy he doesn't know what he's talking about," Mrs. Priddy said, drawing herself up like a heron stalking a frog.

Iva turned to Mr. Priddy. "Mrs. Priddy says you don't know what you're talking about."

"Tell Mrs. Priddy we'll be saddled with Swannanoah till doomsday," he said.

Iva sighed. She'd only come in for a cupcake sample. Now she was stuck giving messages from one Priddy to the other.

Everyone in town knew the Priddys had had a big falling-out. It had happened so long ago, nobody, including them, remembered what it was about. They had not uttered one word to each other in thirty-five years. Not even "Pass the butter."

Iva found this astonishing. The only way

Mr. and Mrs. Priddy communicated was when another person delivered their messages.

Now Mrs. Priddy said to Iva, "Tell *Mr.* Priddy if he wants me to wash his underwear he should put them in the hamper and *not* on the floor."

Iva wanted to giggle, but she turned to Mr. Priddy. "Mrs. Priddy said if you want her to wash—"

"I heard. Iva, tell *Mrs.* Priddy not to hang her stockings from the shower rod. I went into the bathroom the other night and like to strangled myself."

"*Mrs.* Priddy—" Iva began, but Mrs. Priddy waved her away.

"Thanks for coming in, Iva. But as you can see, I'm very busy." She shot a glance at her husband across the aisle. "Too busy to fool with people who will soon be wearing dirty drawers."

Iva gladly headed back outside. Sweetlips got up with a grunt and trotted after her.

"Those two are crazier than a white horse in the moonlight," she said aloud, wondering what they fell out about. The Priddys were different, all right. Not bad-different. Interesting-different.

Instead of going straight home, she headed for the park with the statue of the Uncertain Soldier. The soldier held his rifle by his side, shading his eyes with his other hand. He appeared to be gazing at a distant battlefield.

Iva believed he was looking for a place to hide. Who in their right mind would want to go and get shot at? Look what had happened to General Braddock.

She was more interested in the peach tree growing in the garden. Last night she had read about

Bavaria in a 1928 issue of *National Geographic*. Bavaria was a country where people lived in stone houses and sat around in fancy costumes.

One photo showed a guy with a Y-shaped stick pointed at the ground. He was using the stick to find gold!

"It's called dowsing," Iva said to Sweetlips. She pronounced it "dozing." She broke off a forked branch of the peach tree and stripped off the leaves. "Fruit trees make good dowsing sticks."

She trusted Ludwell's map, but it wouldn't hurt to try something new. She walked slowly with one of the two forked parts of the branch in each hand, and the main stem out in front of her.

"I know Braddock's gold is near the creek," she said. "But I might find a necklace or a ring somebody dropped a long time ago. When I'm near gold, the stick will twitch." She didn't have anything to dig with. If the stick quivered, she'd jam it in the ground to mark the spot, then run home for a shovel.

Sweetlips romped along, hopping up to nip the stick. Iva frowned. "Quit it! We're not playing fetch. This is serious business."

She concentrated so hard on waiting for the stick to quiver, she didn't see Arden and Hunter until they stood right in front of her.

"My sister," Arden said to Hunter, as if Iva were deaf. "Stark, raving bonkers."

"I'm not bonkers," Iva said. "I'm looking for gold. This is my dowsing stick."

"Dozing stick? Hunter, does that stick look asleep?"

"Nope. Seems wide awake to me. But Sweetlips looks drowsy."

Iva waggled her stick in her sister's face. "For your information, the art of dowsing goes back to the days of yore. Only special people can do it."

Arden grabbed the stick and snapped it into twigs. "Don't get in my face ever again." She threw the pieces at Iva's feet. "C'mon, Hunter. Let's go get ice cream."

"When I strike it rich, I'm not giving you one red cent!" Iva yelled as Arden and Hunter walked away, laughing and slapping palms. "Even if you're starving, I wouldn't give you"—she tried to think of the smallest particle of food—"a single celery seed!"

Discouraged, she walked home with her dog. It was too hot to go dowsing anyway.

In her front yard, Iva saw Lily Pearl flapping her arms. Her sister wore their mother's fringed Spanish shawl. Howard crouched on all fours in the grass.

"You're not being a good witch cat," Lily Pearl yelled at him. "Do like this."

She bared her teeth and hissed.

Howard stood up. "I don't want to be a witch cat. I want to be a ghost."

Lily Pearl quit flapping and studied him as if she were going to paint his portrait. "Can you make ghost noises?"

"Oooooh!" Howard moaned. Iva thought

71

he sounded more like he had a stomachache.

"Okay," Lily Pearl said. "You can be a ghost. Now let's go haunt something!" They raced around back, screaming and laughing.

Iva watched them. Her mother's and Aunt Sissy Two's plan to have three sets of double-first cousin girls didn't quite work. Aunt Sissy Two had surprised everybody with a boy to pair up with Lily Pearl. Yet Lily Pearl and Howard were closer than hair on a hog. And you never saw Arden without Hunter.

How come, Iva thought, the other half in *her* set of double-first cousins was such a dud? If only she and Heaven could have a great big falling-out like the Priddys.

Iva pictured a blue line painted on the grass between their houses. Heaven couldn't cross that line. And Iva would never have to speak to her again.

Chapter Six

Baptizing the Cat

Eeeerrk. Sweetlips nosed the screen door open and wiggled through. Iva caught the handle before the door slammed, and eased outside behind him.

"Shhh." She tiptoed across the porch and down the steps. Then she ran like a wild thing toward the shed.

The night before, Iva had decided she'd get up before anyone and go look for Ludwell's treasure. Her family sure wouldn't miss her. And she'd be gone before Heaven came crashing over to wreck her plans. Besides, discoverers always got up at daybreak to go to work.

Iva used to think daybreak made a loud noise,

like a clap of thunder. One night she'd heard a loud thump. She'd run into her parents' room and cried, "Is it dawn yet?"

Her mother had mumbled into her pillow, "It's three in the morning!" The thump turned out to be Lily Pearl falling out of bed.

Iva figured dawn broke at five o'clock, and that was the time she had set her alarm for. But she and Sweetlips woke up before her clock beeped.

Early morning shadows still clung to the corners of the shed. Iva looked around. The pick was missing from its normal spot. Did she leave it on her last exploration? Oh, well. She needed something lighter anyway. She spotted the tall slim handle of a hoe. Her father chopped weeds with it in his vegetable patch, dirt clods flying. That should work.

She balanced the hoe over one shoulder, then set off down the street. Sweetlips frisked along behind her. He held his head high, ears alert. He liked being out early, too.

The morning was as fresh as a new-laid egg.

Iva breathed deeply. The air smelled the way her mother's sheets smelled billowing on the clothesline.

"We should be up at dawn all the time," she told Sweetlips. She tried to whistle but couldn't remember if she was supposed to blow in or out. She blew out, hissing like a flat tire.

They hiked to Henderson's farm on the outskirts of town. Iva made a beeline for the grove of willow trees on the other side of the field. She waded into knee-high purple clover and tasseled ragweed. Sweetlips plowed along beside her like a possum nosing through grapevines.

"I think this is the right place," she said. "Not so close to town." She had worked out this theory in bed last night. General Braddock wouldn't have buried the gold with everybody in Uncertain watching him.

"Let's hurry and find the treasure so I can be famous," she said. She would have her picture in *The Uncertain Star*!

Sweetlips took off. By the time Iva reached the willow trees, he was sitting by Calfpasture Creek as if he'd been waiting for years.

"Very funny," Iva said.

Time to get down to brass tacks. She lined up the sun with the road. Shifting the hoe, she began taking long strides away from the creek.

"One, two, three, four—"

A faint cry came from upstream.

Iva dropped the hoe and froze. What was that? It sounded like a wild animal!

THE UNCERTAI

Monday, August 1st

Local Discoverer Iva Honeysuckle Solves Mystery, Finds Treasure

Iva says that she first became aware of the possible location of the treasure after finding an old journal that had belonged to her grandfather and had been used originally to record tire preasure. When asked what her next adventure might involve, Miss Honeysuckle declared that she would be traveling to the north edge of

Discoverers faced danger all the time. They wrestled with crocodiles and dodged charging rhinos. It was part of the job.

Maybe it was a vicious boa constrictor. Iva had always wanted to fight a boa constrictor. Did boa constrictors have lips? Could they make noises?

"We must do this!" said a human voice.

Definitely not a boa constrictor. The voice sounded familiar. . . .

Sweetlips lifted his nose, sniffing the slight breeze. Baying, he bolted into the creek. "*A-rooooo!*"

"Get back here!" Iva yelled.

Sweetlips ran as if he smelled the biggest plate of liver and onions in the universe.

Iva kicked off her sneakers and splashed after him. "Some faithful discoverer dog you are!"

The water was shallow this time of year, barely up to her ankles. Iva flailed upstream, trying not to slip on moss-slick stones. She rounded the bend, then stopped.

Heaven stood in the middle of the creek. She cradled a doll in one arm.

The new-laid day suddenly turned rotten. Iva couldn't believe it. What was *Heaven* doing in the exact same place *she* was? And why did she have a doll?

The doll wore a white lace dress. A white lace cap was jammed on its head. Two ears poked up from holes cut in the cap, and the tip of a brown-and-orange tail switched beneath the long skirt.

It was Yard Sale.

"Please!" Heaven begged. "Just a few teensy drips and we can go home, I promise." She leaned toward the water. The cat arched its back like a croquet wicket.

Sweetlips bounded up and smacked his muddy paws on Heaven's legs. He had never seen a cat in a dress before. Yard Sale spat at him and clawed up Heaven's arm.

"Go away, you stupid dog!" Heaven yelled. Sweetlips danced around her, eager to play.

Iva sloshed over. "Heaven!"

"Get that mutt out of here!"

"He's just trying to save your cat!"

"*I'm* trying to save my cat!" Heaven breathed damply into Iva's face. "Get her loose, will you? She's scratching me."

Iva gently unhooked Yard Sale's toenails from Heaven's collar. "What on earth are you *doing*?"

Heaven snatched the cat away. "What does it look like? I'm baptizing her."

Iva was so astonished, all she could say was, "Immersion or sprinkle?"

"Sprinkle. You think I'd be crazy enough to dunk a cat?" Heaven puffed indignantly through her left nostril.

Yard Sale's tuft of orange fur bristled from beneath the white cap. Iva felt sorry for her. "Why are you torturing this poor cat?"

"I'm baptizing her so Mama can't make me get rid of her."

"Did she find Yard Sale in your room?" Iva felt a bubble of pleasure. High time Heaven got in trouble.

"No, but Howard's been sneezing something awful," Heaven said. "If I baptize Yard Sale, then she'll be a member of the family. And Mama will have to let me keep her."

"Do you really think Aunt Sissy Two will—" Iva saw her dog bunching his hind legs to spring. "Sweetlips! No!"

Too late. Sweetlips leaped and nipped Yard Sale's tail. Yard Sale squirted out of Heaven's arms like a greased minnow. She landed on the other side of the creek and scrabbled up the nearest tree.

Heaven screamed.

Sweetlips *a-roo*ed and chased after the cat.

Yard Sale climbed higher.

"*Do* something!" Heaven shrieked, floundering to the other side of the creek.

Iva minced across, stepping on each stone carefully. She wasn't about to rush. For the first time in the history of the world, Heaven needed her.

Heaven hopped up and down. *"Hurry!"* Heaven was having a hissy fit with a tail on it. Iva knew why her cousin was so frantic.

Last summer they had climbed Miz Compton's mimosa tree to pick the frilly pink blossoms. Iva had planned to tie an army man to hers and drop it like a parachute. Heaven wanted to make ballerina dancers.

Iva had shinnied up the trunk, nimble as a monkey. Heaven had huffed and struggled to the first slender branch. It snapped like a toothpick, and she hit the ground on her butt. From then on, Heaven refused to climb a tree.

"What will you give me if I get her down?" Iva said, buffing her nails on her shirt.

"Anything!"

Iva thought. She didn't want Heaven's framed certificates for perfect attendance at Sunday school. She didn't want a bottle of toilet water from Heaven's collection. She certainly didn't want a tea towel from Heaven's Hope Drawer.

There was only one thing of Heaven's that Iva truly wanted.

"If I get her down," she said, "can I have her? Your mother won't let you keep a pet, so you might as well give her to me."

Heaven's gray eyes slid away from Iva's. "Sure. Just get her down."

"Hold Sweetlips so he won't scare Yard Sale any worse."

Heaven hauled Sweetlips away by his collar.

Iva jumped up and snagged the lowest branch of the tree. She hung for a few seconds, then swung up. Her bare toes gripped each branch as she climbed.

Yard Sale crouched above her. Her orange eyes flashed fire.

"Nice kitty," Iva said soothingly. She stretched her hand out. "Co-o-ome here."

Yard Sale tensed. Iva grabbed the hem of the cat's dress and scooped her up. Yard Sale dug her claws into Iva's neck. Iva gritted her teeth as she scrambled back down.

Heaven reached up and took the cat. "Poor baby!"

Iva dropped heavily to the ground. "What about me?" She rubbed her stinging neck. "Okay, hand her over."

"No."

Heat rose in Iva like mercury in a thermometer. "You stinker! A deal's a deal!"

"My fingers were crossed behind my back," Heaven said. "So it doesn't count. Anyway, I changed my mind. I'm keeping her."

"I'm telling Aunt Sissy Two! That cat can't live at your house!"

"She won't have to. Miz Compton said I could keep Yard Sale at her house," Heaven said. "She told me that when she helped me buy her at Cazy Sparkle's."

"You say!"

"I do say! *And* Miz Compton told me I can visit my cat anytime I want." With Yard Sale over her shoulder, Heaven walked toward the road.

Iva boiled over with anger. How dare Heaven get to keep the cat and steal her best friend! "You can't have everything your way, Heaven Honeycutt!"

Heaven lifted Yard Sale's paw in a little wave.

Iva bent down by the creek to throw water on her face before she had a stroke. She was wrong. Heaven *did* always get everything her way.

That was going to change.

Chapter Seven

The Great Flannel-Board Incident

Iva dipped the tip of her spoon in her Cream of Wheat and ate the tiniest possible bite. Her mother *would* fix that awful cereal today of all days.

Her mother banged a plate of toast on the paper-littered table. "Don't let breakfast get cold."

Arden was slumped over her latest creation, a Johnny Cash–type song called "Uncertain Prison Blues."

"I can't eat," she said. "I'm doing hard time in Uncertain Prison."

"What do you think of this?" Hunter said. She was writing a Nancy Drew mystery, *The Secret of the Haunted Sewer Drain*. "'The pretty blond detective answered the jangling telephone. "Come at once," a deep voice cried exultantly.'"

"'Exultantly'?" Iva jeered. "Do you even know what that means?"

"Who taught that kid to talk?" Arden said. "Okay, my turn." She began singing. "I hear the bus a'comin'. I know it ain't for me. I'm stuck in this here prison. The sun I'll never see."

Iva fell over laughing. "'The sun I'll never see'? You must be kidding!"

Arden punched her on the arm. Iva whacked her back.

"Girls," their mother warned. "Lily Pearl! Where are you?"

Lily Pearl whirled in, wearing last year's Halloween costume. Her skinny legs stuck out like twigs beneath the too-short purple dress. Green stars glittered on the matching purple cape.

"You are *not* wearing that getup to vacation church school," Mrs. Honeycutt said. "Go change right this minute."

"No." Lily Pearl's bottom lip poked out.

"I'm counting to three. One, two—"

Lily Pearl started to bawl. "These are my bestest clothes!"

"Do you want to go to vacation church school or not?" Mrs. Honeycutt said.

Iva wished *she* had thought of putting on a Halloween costume to get out of going to church school.

"Listen, Lily Pearl," Iva said. "Why don't you leave the cape at home? That way people can see your pretty dress."

Lily Pearl's tears vanished like water in sand. "Okay, Mama?"

"All right. But don't tell anybody it's a Halloween costume."

Mrs. Honeycutt set a bowl of Cream of Wheat

in front of Lily Pearl. Lily Pearl just twirled her spoon.

"Eat!" her mother said. "No wonder you're no bigger than a bar of soap on wash day."

The back door opened and Aunt Sissy Two came in with Howard. Howard's white shirt was so bright it hurt Iva's eyes. Comb tracks raked his slicked-back hair.

"Here we are. All ready for church school!" Then Aunt Sissy Two said to Iva's mother, "Howard's over that allergy attack. I don't know what brought it on."

Iva knew. She thought about tattling on Heaven, but since Yard Sale was at Miz Compton's, there wasn't any point.

"How come Arden and Hunter don't have to go?" she asked.

"Because vacation church school is for babies," Arden said. She sang in her low-down Johnny Cash voice, "I spend all night a'cryin'. I got the Uncertain Pri-son blues."

"Go on, Iva. You'll all be late," her mother said. "Arden, there is no prison in Uncertain."

Yes, there is, Iva thought. She followed Lily Pearl and Howard outside and headed for the Joyful Noise Temple of Deliverance Church.

The Sunday-school room was stuffy and hot and smelled like old socks. Heaven greeted everyone with a stiff nod. Iva felt as if she were in the principal's office.

Fidgety little kids sat in all but three of the small wooden chairs. Lily Pearl and Howard fought over the chair by the stained-glass window.

Iva turned to Heaven. "I thought more kids our age were coming."

"Nobody our age signed up but you," Heaven said, arranging colored pencils next to a stack of dreary-looking worksheets.

"I didn't sign up! Mama signed me up because of you!"

"You're here now. Sit down so we can start."

Iva flumped down in the last chair. Her knees bumped her chin. She was the biggest one in the class.

Miz Compton breezed into the room with a big smile.

"Good morning," she said. "Welcome to vacation church school. We're going to have lots of fun today. Heaven, would you pass out the activity sheets?"

"Yes, ma'am."

Heaven handed out papers with an air of grandness that made Iva sick. When Miz Compton wasn't looking, Heaven tossed the last sheet at Iva, then flounced to the front of the room.

The little kids studied their papers as if they were taking a test.

"First, cut out the boy and the wagon," Miz Compton instructed.

"Then paste them on the middle of your paper. We'll have to share scissors and paste."

Iva stared at the blurry boy printed on the cheap grainy paper. He looked like he had three eyes. She ripped the paper, using scissors that wouldn't dent melted butter.

"Give me that," Iva said to Howard, who was eating paste straight from the jar. She swiped sticky paste on the back of the blurry boy and his stupid wagon, and smacked them down with her fist.

"Next, color your pictures," Miz Compton said brightly.

Heaven doled out colored pencils with a warning not to break them. When she got to Iva, she dropped a single chewed pencil in her lap. Chestnut brown.

"I need more than one," Iva said, but Heaven was already collecting the scissors.

Iva scribble-scrabbled her picture with the chestnut-brown pencil. She didn't even try to stay inside the lines.

"Heaven has chosen our quote for the day," Miz Compton said. "*Be a friend, find a friend.* Isn't that wonderful?"

Heaven glowed like the angel in the stained-glass window. Iva was surprised she didn't sprout wings and start playing a harp.

Miz Compton wrote the saying in large, neat letters on the blackboard. The little kids copied the words slowly. Iva noticed Howard made his *f*'s and *r*'s backward. Lily Pearl drew a witch in a ball gown riding in the wagon.

Iva pressed the tip of her pencil so hard into the paper, it snapped. Leave it to Heaven to pick such a dumb saying. What did *she* know about being a friend? And what did the quote have to do with the picture? Was the wagon the boy's friend?

It was all so dumb. Iva *had* to get out of vacation church school.

"You may take your papers home," Miz Compton said. "After our snack, we'll have our flannel-board story. Heaven, will you get the board ready?"

Heaven glanced longingly at the wood-framed flannel board. Iva knew Heaven's greatest wish was to have a flannel board of her own.

"But first," Miz Compton told Heaven, "take everyone to the washroom."

"Line up by the door," Heaven ordered the little kids. "We'll be right back all shiny clean!" she trilled to Miz Compton. Then she marched the kids down the hall.

Iva nearly gagged. Her cousin was putting on an act. If only Miz Compton could see Heaven was no angel.

Miz Compton spoke to her. "Iva, would you like to help with the refreshments?"

Iva had an idea. Now was her opportunity to show her best friend that Heaven was a big fat fake. *This* time, Heaven wouldn't get her own way.

"In a minute," Iva said. "I have to use the restroom, too."

When Miz Compton went into the little church kitchen, Iva sprang out of her seat. She opened the box of soft flannel figures and dumped them on the desk.

First she slapped a flannel palm tree in the middle of the board. Grabbing a handful of people, she stuck them on the palm tree. Zacchaeus the tax collector. Moses. The Three Wise Men. Noah. Joseph wearing his coat of many colors.

Then Iva added all the animals from Noah's ark. She snickered as she put a lion on Moses's head. The Three Wise Men were being attacked by an alligator.

Flannel figures covered the board to the edges of the wooden frame. With a dab of paste, Iva glued a few Pharisees and Philistines to the frame for good measure.

When she heard Lily Pearl's shrill voice, Iva dashed into the kitchen, where Miz Compton was pouring Hawaiian Punch into paper cups.

"There you are," Miz Compton said. "Will you take the cookies in?"

"Sure." Iva picked up the platter and carried it into the classroom. Miz Compton followed with the tray of Hawaiian Punch.

Heaven stood in front of the flannel board. One of the flannel Philistines hung limply from her fingers. The little kids skittered around her, nervous as chipmunks.

"Look!" Heaven cried.

Miz Compton set the tray on her desk and stared at the flannel board. "Goodness gracious! Who would do such a thing?"

"Yeah, who?" Iva said, pretending to sound shocked.

"It wasn't me," Heaven said. "I was with the kids in the bathroom."

"Not the whole time," Lily Pearl piped up. "Remember? Howard and James went in by themselves."

"I saw Heaven in here a minute ago," Iva said to Miz Compton. "Before the kids came back." She made her eyes round with innocence.

"You *lie*!" Heaven screeched.

"A skunk smells himself first." Iva snuck a couple of cookies. Getting Heaven into trouble was giving her an appetite.

"Who are you calling a skunk, you rat!"

"Heaven and Iva," Miz Compton said sternly. "There is no cause for that talk."

"Iva's jealous because I'm your assistant," Heaven said. "She's trying to get me fired from my job!"

"Oh, shut up about your stupid job."

Miz Compton turned to Iva. Her voice was soft but firm. "Iva, apologize to Heaven."

"Why? *She* messed up the flannel board!"

"*Iva.*"

Iva blinked back a sudden welling of tears. Her trick hadn't worked. "I won't apologize to her, not in a million years!"

"I don't think your attitude is right for church school," Miz Compton said. "Maybe you should go home."

There was nothing else to say. Iva glared at Heaven, who was removing the flannel people and animals and laying them tenderly on the desk.

Sunlight poured through the stained-glass window. The angel's halo seemed to shimmer around Heaven's head.

Iva pushed past her and ran out of the church. Her mother would probably kill her for flunking out of vacation church school.

At least she wouldn't have to go back.

Chapter Eight

Swannanoah's Dump

Iva tried slipping through the gate like a rubber snake. She hoped to slink inside the house and hole up in her room until church school was over. It didn't work.

Her mother was planted in the rocking chair on the porch, an old enameled basin in her lap. Beside her, a peck basket overflowed with fresh-picked lima beans. She snapped each shell and flicked the beans into the basin with one smooth movement.

Sweetlips lay at her feet. He raised his head when he saw Iva coming down the sidewalk.

Both Iva's dog and Iva's mother frowned with disapproval.

"Hi, Mama," Iva said with a cheerful smile. "Church school's out early, being it's the first day and all."

Her mother tossed an empty hull in a bucket. "Then where are Lily Pearl and Howard? Where's Heaven?"

"Um . . . they're staying after for extra credit." Iva let her mouth fall a little slack, a technique she had perfected. A tense jaw was a sure sign of fibbing.

Lima beans pattered into the pan. "Iva, I know you were told to leave."

Who squealed? And how had the news gotten back to her mother so quick? Even Heaven couldn't tattle faster than the speed of light.

"Everybody is in everybody else's back pocket in this town." Mrs. Honeycutt looked at Iva. "*Nobody* gets expelled from vacation church school!"

"Don't you always say there's a first time for everything?" Iva said, with a weak laugh.

"At least you owned up to it." Her mother pushed the basket toward Iva. "I'm disappointed in you. You deliberately tried to get your cousin into trouble."

Iva hated shelling limas. The tough hulls hurt her hands. She slit open one end of a pod, ran her thumb inside the damp waxy shell, and popped out four pale green beans.

Plunk, plunk. Her mother hulled like she was unzipping a zipper. "I'm not going to ask you why you did it, because that's beside the point. What do you think you should do?"

"Apologize to Miz Compton?" Iva hoped this would be enough.

"Anyone else?"

"Heaven too. I guess," she added slowly. She would rather crawl fifty miles over broken glass than tell Heaven she was sorry. "Are we having creamed lima beans for supper?" she said, to change the subject.

"I want you to make things right this evening,"

her mother said. "I'll see Walser Compton at circle meeting tonight. If you haven't apologized by then—"

"I will, I will."

Iva had no intention of going to Miz Compton's this afternoon. She had tried to show Miz Compton that Heaven was a phony. Instead, she had wound up making herself look terrible and losing the only friend she had. She had never felt worse in her entire life.

Arden and Hunter bounced down the steps.

"You flunked vacation church school!" Arden crowed. "That takes special talent."

"Which is more than you have," Iva fired back.

It was impossible to keep a secret in this town. Everybody *was* in everybody else's back pocket.

Iva checked the pocket of her shorts. It would be like just like Heaven to shrink herself teeny-tiny so Iva would unknowingly carry her around, like a germ.

* * *

At the end of a gravel road just outside of town rose a mammoth pile of trash. The town dump was ruled by Swannanoah Priddy, owner of the fastest pickup truck in Uncertain. The gleaming yellow truck was parked snugly by Swannanoah's little house.

Iva often went to the dump when she needed to think. Nobody there made her go to church school or yelled at her or tattled on her. It was peaceful. Old trees shaded the parking lot. A tiny creek trickled at the bottom of the hill.

On one side, garbage was heaped like a gigantic ice cream sundae. Hemmed in by a low wall, castoffs like stoves and lawn mowers paraded along the other side.

Iva crossed the lot. Sweetlips trotted along with his nose so close to the ground, Iva worried he would suck gravel up his nostrils.

Swannanoah was sorting through a big cardboard box. Even though it was hotter than smoke from a locomotive, she wore her year-round

uniform of men's dungarees and a flannel shirt. She once told Iva she didn't need to dress up to wade through coffee grounds and oil rags.

"Hey, Swan," Iva said. "Anything new come in?"

"Just put some stuff out."

Swannanoah rescued the better things people threw away and set them on the wall above a sign that said *Somebody's Trash Is Another Person's Treasure.*

Iva was amazed at what people got rid of. Propped against the wall today was a perfectly good picture of a crying clown painted on black velvet. Next to that was a fancy silver thing that covered a telephone. A make-up present for Miz Compton?

And then she saw it. A hefty square of canvas with two rusty poles sticking out.

An army pup tent.

Iva clutched her chest. Every discoverer needed a tent. It was a requirement. They could hardly check into a motel if they were thrashing around in the wilderness.

"Swan! Can I have the tent?"

"If you can carry it off under your own steam, it's yours."

Iva lifted the canvas. It smelled like mildew, and one corner was torn. She wondered if a grizzly bear had ripped it with his huge paw. The tent had probably been in a lot of adventures. And now it was hers!

Euple Free purred up in The Truck. He switched off the engine, hopped out, and gently shut The Truck's door.

"Hey, Iva," he said. "Hey, Miss Swan."

Swannanoah punched him on the arm. "Hey, yourself, Euple Free."

They chatted about the blistering heat, Euple's pepper patch, Swannanoah's trip to Natural Bridge.

Iva stared at them. Last summer Swannanoah had beat the tar out of Euple in that race. If Iva had been him, she wouldn't give Swannanoah Priddy the pits from her prunes. Not that Iva ever ate prunes.

Euple echoed Iva's question. "Anything new?"

"Something came in just yesterday. The minute I laid eyes on it, I thought, I know a pickup that needs this." She pointed to a shiny object sitting on a busted stove.

Euple ambled on over. Sweetlips trotted behind him, snuffling every inch of the way. Iva's dog loved the dump as much as she did.

"How come you and Euple are so chummy?" Iva asked Swannanoah. "After you beat him and all."

"Why, Iva, Eupe and me was friends long before the race. We played in the sandbox together. Why shouldn't we be friends now?"

"Seems like you'd be enemies, I'm just saying."

"Let me tell you something, Iva. If I thought Euple wouldn't speak to me if I won that race instead of him, I would never have put my truck in gear. Life is too short to spend it mad at somebody."

Iva thought about Swannanoah's parents. They'd spent the last thirty-five years mad at each other. People in town laughed at Mr. and Mrs. Priddy, but Swannanoah probably didn't think it was so funny. Imagine growing up with parents like that.

Euple held up a silver statue of a panther. "Woo-hoo!"

"Look at him, grinning to beat the band," Swannanoah said, grinning herself. "That hood ornament's a beaut."

"How come you don't want it for *your* truck?" Iva asked.

"Because I knew Euple would be tickled over

it. Well, this work isn't doing itself." She dragged another box over and emptied it.

Euple came back, buffing the panther on his shirttail. "The Truck will be proud to wear this!"

"Look what I found today." Iva showed him the pup tent.

Euple admired the tent. "You could go camping."

Iva didn't tell him she wouldn't set up the tent for something so undignified. Her tent would be used for discoverer business only.

"You know, a famous person camped here once," Euple said. "General Braddock."

"*The* General Braddock?" Iva exclaimed. "How do you know about him?"

"I study up on things. Wars, mostly. The French and Indian War is my favorite war."

She nodded. "Mine too."

Euple pointed to an enormous oak tree near the creek. "That tree was a stripling when Braddock and his men camped here. You know who was with them?"

"Who?"

"George Washington. He was real young. Head of the Virginia militia. The militia was with Braddock's outfit."

Iva nearly swooned. Her hero had stood in this very spot! Maybe fixed his own breakfast. She could practically smell bacon sizzling over a campfire.

"Did they have a battle here?" she asked.

Euple shook his head. "Just camped for a few days. Braddock was in a mighty big hurry to get to Pennsylvania to fight the French. I often wonder why they stayed here so long."

Iva knew. General Braddock needed to bury that heavy war chest.

"Well, The Truck is anxious to try on his new hat," Euple said. "Catch y'all later."

Iva was thinking about the clues on Ludwell's map . . . *50 paces east of a stream, where the road runs North and South.*

She tipped her head back so fast her neck cracked. The sun was setting to the right of the dump road. That was west. The dump road must run north and south!

The tree! She ran to the big old oak tree. The creek mumbled behind her. It was all just like the map said!

Iva shivered in the hot sun. This was the best day! First she found the pup tent. And now she had solved the last clue on Ludwell's map. None of this would have happened if she hadn't gotten thrown out of vacation church school.

Now Great Discoverer Iva Honeysuckle briskly counted off her steps. Too bad a photographer wasn't there to record her great moment.

She thought about how she'd pose for her picture in *The Uncertain Star*. Maybe she'd sit on the cannon as if she were riding a horse. No! She'd stack all those shiny beautiful gold coins into layers like Swannanoah's bride's cake.

Don't lose track. "Ten, eleven, twelve . . ."

Up the hill, past a stump. "Twenty-seven, twenty-eight . . ."

Around the edge of the parking lot. "Forty-four, forty-five . . ."

Famous discoverer Iva Honeysuckle stopped dead.

The mountain of trash loomed before her. Banana peels, orange skins, doughnut boxes, bread crusts, tea bags, used Kleenexes, dog-food cans, half-eaten tuna sandwiches—all of it heated by the scorching sun and reeking to high heaven.

Braddock's gold was buried under the garbage from the town of Uncertain.

Chapter Nine

Iva's Grand Plan

When Iva heard her mother's car door slam, she hopped into bed and switched off the light. The front door squeaked shut.

"Lily Pearl." Her mother's voice carried down the hall into Iva's room. "Pick up every one of those Cheerios and get in the bed. Arden, help her with her pajamas."

Arden mumbled something Iva couldn't make out. Then she heard her mother's measured tread heading down the hall toward her room.

Iva shoved Sweetlips to the foot of her bed and lay on her side with her arm hanging off the mattress. She closed her eyes and breathed evenly and naturally.

Bright light fell across the rug as her mother came in. Sweetlips thumped his tail.

Her mother leaned over and tucked Iva's arm under the covers. Then she tiptoed out. Before she eased the door shut, she said, "We'll talk in the morning, missy."

Iva sat up. She hadn't fooled her mother one bit! Well, at least she wouldn't have to face the music until tomorrow about why she hadn't apologized to Miz Compton. Meanwhile, Iva had some planning to do.

She switched on her nightstand light and pulled the flimsy Uncertain phone book out from under the covers. Riffling through the pages, she stopped at a listing for Acme Bulldozers. *Rent-a-dozer, fifty dollars an hour.*

Iva had sixty-three cents, and she owed thirty cents of that to Arden. She doubted her mother would loan her forty-nine dollars and . . . sixty-seven cents. And she doubted the rent-a-dozer man would let an almost-nine-year-old girl drive his bulldozer, even if Iva did have the money.

She tossed the phone book on the floor. *How* would she dig under all that trash to get to the treasure? She wasn't strong enough to do it by herself. Much as she hated to admit it, she needed a partner. But who?

Miz Compton. She was Iva's closest friend. She'd ask her nephew Peter, owner of the second-fastest pickup and editor of *The Uncertain Star*, to dig the hole for Iva. Iva would give him one of the gold coins as payment.

Tomorrow after church school, Iva would go to Miz Compton's and tell her she was sorry about the flannel-board incident. After they'd made up over unsweetened cherry Kool-Aid and preacher cookies, Iva would tell Miz Compton she needed Peter's help. Now *that* was a plan.

If her mother and Aunt Sissy Two could have a grand plan, so could Iva.

As she cut her light out, Iva noticed Heaven's lamp was still on. Heaven was probably choosing the dumb quote for the day for church school tomorrow. *Be a friend, find a friend.*

Yeah, right.

Iva sailed up Miz Compton's sidewalk, filled with breezy confidence. She rapped the brass lion's-head knocker twice, and smiled so all her teeth showed. She'd read in one of Ludwell's *National*

Geographic magazines that if you show all your teeth when you smile, people who don't speak your language know you're friendly.

The door swung open, and Heaven stood there. Iva's toothy smile slipped sideways.

"What are you doing here?" she asked Heaven.

"Visiting Yard Sale. And helping with tomorrow's craft," Heaven replied. "What are *you* doing here?"

"I came to see Miz Compton. Let me in."

Heaven started to shut the door. From somewhere within the house, Miz Compton called, "Who is it, Heaven?"

"Nobody," Heaven called over her shoulder.

Iva was in no mood. Because she hadn't apologized to Miz Compton the evening before, Iva had spent the morning weeding the cucumber patch and swatting gnats.

She pushed past Heaven as Miz Compton came in from the dining room.

"Iva," she said. "How nice of you to drop by."

"*Un*announced." Heaven placed her fists on her hips. "*Some* people are busy."

Iva ignored her. "Miz Compton . . . uh . . ." Her breezy confidence popped like a balloon. She couldn't ask Miz Compton to be her partner with Heaven's big self there.

"Heaven," Miz Compton said. "Let Iva see our craft project."

Our project? Now Heaven was doing projects with Iva's best friend?

"Come on," Heaven said, none too graciously. Iva followed her into the kitchen.

Yard Sale was curled up in a sewing basket, one white-tipped paw draped over the side.

"Awww," Iva said.

"Miz Compton fixed her a bed, but Yard Sale was bound and determined to sleep in her sewing basket." Heaven petted Yard Sale's little head. "So Miz Compton had to take her needles and thread out."

"Okay," Iva said. "Let's see this big project."

"Here it is."

Mason jars lined the countertop, each filled with bendy stems of Queen Anne's lace, the white-flowered weed found along roadsides. The water in each of the jars was a different color: bright blue, yellow, green, and pink.

"You put food coloring in the water," Heaven said. "And then you stick the Queen Anne's lace in and leave it overnight. The flowers turn the color of the water!"

It was true. The white flowers were now pink and green and pale yellow and a soft sky blue. Iva had never seen such a neat trick.

"So what?" she said. "I mean, you can get flowers that are already colored."

"The little kids will

think it's a big deal," Heaven said, straightening the stem of a pink flower. "Every day Miz Compton and me plan a new project." She smiled, showing only her front teeth.

A false smile, Iva thought. People who couldn't speak her language wouldn't be fooled a second.

Miz Compton came in to fetch a jar of furniture polish from the cupboard. She struggled with the lid. "Heaven, dear, can you open this?"

Dear! Miz Compton never called Iva *dear.*

"Sure." Heaven untwisted the cap with ease.

"Isn't she amazing, Iva?" Miz Compton said.

Heaven crooked her arm and patted her muscle.

"Yeah," Iva said. "Amazing." She had to move things along. Obviously she wouldn't be making up with Miz Compton over Kool-Aid and preacher cookies. Not with "Heaven, dear" sniffing around.

"Can I talk to you?" Iva asked Miz Compton.

"Someplace *private*."

"I'll go pick out tomorrow's coloring sheet," Heaven said carelessly.

"Thank you, dear. Iva and I will go out on the porch."

Iva and Miz Compton went outside and sat in the rocking chairs.

"Now. Iva, what's on your mind?"

"I'm sorry about yesterday. The flannel board and all. I mean it."

"I thought that might be it. And I accept your apology. Let's put it behind us, shall we?"

"Okay." Iva felt damp with relief. The hard part was over. "There's something else. . . . You know that thing I've been hunting for all summer?"

As Miz Compton rocked, she fanned herself with one hand. "You never told me exactly what it was. Did you find it?"

"Almost," Iva said. "I need—well, first I should tell you about it. You know that stuff Daddy gave me that belonged to his grandfather? Ludwell Honeycutt?"

She nodded. "Some old *National Geographic* magazines and things."

"Well, I was reading one of the magazines one night, and this map fell out. Ludwell wrote it— it's got clues to a hidden treasure!"

"Is that right?" Miz Compton's voice had that downward turn grown-ups used when they didn't really believe you.

Iva barreled on, anyway. "See, General Braddock had to get rid of the gold he had because it was too heavy, and he had to go fight the French in Pennsylvania. When he camped here—Euple Free told me this, so I know it's true—he buried the gold in a cannon. Right here in Uncertain! And he wrote a map with the directions."

"The same map in Ludwell's magazine?"

"Not the *same* map, because it's in Ludwell's handwriting." Sometimes grown-ups, even good ones like Miz Compton, should pay attention more. "Anyway, I've been looking and looking. And yesterday I finally found the spot!"

Miz Compton stopped rocking. "You found the gold?"

"No, I found the *spot* where the gold is buried," Iva explained. "It's under— something real heavy. Would you ask Peter to dig the hole for me? He's strong."

"I'm afraid Peter is at a newspaper convention in Myrtle Beach."

"How about you?" Iva said. "I'll pay you! The map says General Braddock buried thirty thousand pounds in gold. A pound is sort of like our dollar. And that was back in the seventeen hundreds! Who knows what it's worth today?"

Miz Compton smiled. Iva tried to count her teeth to see if it was a real friendly smile or a fake friendly smile, but Miz Compton was talking. "I wouldn't be much use in your treasure hunt. I can't even twist the lid off a jar of furniture polish!"

Iva started to cry. Her grand plan was a bust. Worse, Miz Compton and "Heaven, dear" were closer than boll weevils on a cotton stalk.

"Iva, don't take on so. I'm sorry I can't help you—" Miz Compton leaned forward, concerned.

"That's not it!" Iva swiped at her tears. "Well, not all of it. You aren't my friend anymore."

"Of course I'm your friend," she said.

"No, you aren't!" Iva said unreasonably. "I don't have a single solitary friend in the whole world."

"Iva," Miz Compton said gently. "You go around like you don't *need* any friends. And you don't see the people right in front of you who could be your friends. Remember the quote Heaven wrote yesterday—"

"Not that stupid quote again!"

"—if you *are* a friend, you'll *have* a friend." She patted Iva's shoulder. "I'll let you get yourself together while I fix us something cool to drink." She went inside the house.

Iva looked up.

Heaven stood in the doorway, staring at Iva. Her strong jar-twisting arms hung by her sides. Her sturdy tanned legs were planted like trees. Her ladies'-sized feet were splayed out like roots.

In that instant, Iva knew two things. She knew that Heaven had overheard her talking about Braddock's gold.

And she knew she needed Heaven to help her find it.

Chapter Ten

Braddock's Gold

"Heaven!" Iva tried to make her voice light. "How long have you been standing there?"

"Long enough." Heaven came out on the porch.

"I was just going to ask—"

"I know what you're going to ask," Heaven said flatly. "I want half the treasure."

"Half! But I've done all the work! I figured out the clues . . . and I've looked all summer for the right spot. How about—" Iva calculated quickly. How many people had she promised to give gold to? At this rate, she wouldn't have any treasure left. Still, she needed Heaven.

"How about a hundred dollars?" she said.

Heaven folded her arms. "Half. And I want to be a full partner."

"*I'm* the discoverer. Only *one* person can make a great discovery." She could still be a member of the National Geographic Society, but her cousin would want to horn in on that too.

"No dice." Heaven headed back inside.

Iva practically leaped across the porch. Heaven was her last chance.

"Wait! Okay, you can have half the gold." It was only money, Iva thought with a pang. The important thing was that she had found Ludwell's treasure. "And you can be my partner, but you have to be a *silent* partner."

"What does that mean?"

"It means you can't talk about it. It's my discovery," Iva said. Sensing Heaven was backing off again, she added, "Fifteen thousand dollars will buy a *lot* of pot holders and embroidered pillowcases."

"Deal," Heaven said. "I'll tell Miz Compton we're leaving."

Iva knew she had made the right decision. Heaven might be a pain, but nothing stopped that girl when she made up her mind to do something.

Heaven came out of the house and clipped briskly down the steps.

"There's a lamp I want to get at Cazy Sparkle's yard sale tomorrow," she said. "The shade is a clear plastic tub with butterflies. You put it on your TV, and the warmth from the TV makes the tub go around. The butterflies look like they're flying." She shot Iva a meaningful glance. "I want it bad."

A sharp pain flickered through Iva's right temple. The treasure had better be there. She hated to think what Heaven would do to her if it wasn't.

Heaven dropped the shovel Iva had borrowed from her father's shed, and waved her arms at the mountain of steaming garbage.

"The *dump*?" she exclaimed. "*This* is where that old guy buried the gold?"

"It wasn't the dump back when General Braddock was here," Iva told her. "It was a pretty field with trees and flowers."

"Well, it's not so pretty now," Heaven said with disgust.

Iva had planned to find the treasure in an hour or so, before the worst heat of the day. Her picture would be splashed across the front page of the evening edition of *The Uncertain Star.*

But by the time she and Heaven had walked to Iva's house to get the shovel, and then stopped at Heaven's house because Heaven wanted a brown-sugar-and-butter sandwich, and Iva decided she wanted one, too, and then walked all the way to the dump, the sun was at its sizzling midafternoon peak.

Stinky steam rose from the garbage pile.

Iva glanced up the road at Swannanoah

Priddy's little house. Swannanoah was working on the engine of her yellow pickup truck. She didn't see Iva and Heaven sneak across the parking lot.

"How do you know this is the right place? Where's the map?" Heaven demanded. "I want to see it."

"I don't have it with me. I memorized the clues," Iva said. "Trust me, this is the spot."

"Can we get started?" Heaven asked. "Before I have a heat stroke?"

"Excuse me, please." Iva brushed past Heaven. "I need to pace off again."

She marched to the old oak tree, turned smartly, and began counting out loud as she strode toward the dump. Up the hill, past the stump, across the parking lot.

She stopped at the very edge of the garbage mound.

Forty-five steps. Same as last time. She estimated another five steps inside the garbage heap, picked up a rock, and placed it in the center of a particularly ripe pile of used kitty litter.

"Start digging right here," Iva said.

Heaven stabbed the shovel downward, like a spear. She scooped up a shovelful of kitty litter and expertly tossed it over her left shoulder.

"You could do this for a living," Iva said. Discoverers were supposed to praise their workers. It made them feel good.

"Let's see if this shovel fits in your mouth."

"Ha-ha!" Iva stepped back, just in case.

Heaven dug and dug. She cleared out used Kleenexes, burned toast, moldy hot-dog buns, and what looked like a mess of beef stew that somebody had eaten and then spit out.

She dug through onion peels, watermelon rinds, corn cobs, green cheese, and a squashed birthday cake. Iva decided she would never eat again.

After a while, Heaven said testily, "How far down is this so-called treasure?"

"Just a foot." Iva peered into the soupy hole Heaven had dug so far.

"A foot starting *where*?" Heaven asked. "How far down does the garbage pit go before it's regular ground?"

"Not too far," Iva said, though she didn't really know. "If we dig a little more, we should hit real dirt, and then it'll be a foot down from that."

"What's this *we* stuff?" Heaven said. "When are *you* going to take a turn?"

Iva pretended she didn't hear. "Ludwell's map said General Braddock buried the gold in a cannon sticking up. The end had a wooden plug in it."

"Yeah? So?"

"I think the hole should be wider." Iva spaced her hands apart. "Like this. That way we have a better chance of finding the cannon."

Heaven actually agreed. "Makes sense." She went back to digging, widening the hole. Soon she said, "I hit red dirt."

The red clay General Braddock wrote about, Iva thought. "Keep going!" she said encouragingly.

Heaven dug and dug and dug. "Okay. This is one foot down."

"How do you know?" Iva asked.

"I have a ruler leg."

"A what?" Iva wondered if the sun was making Heaven funny in the head.

"Remember when we were studying inches and feet and all that stuff?" Heaven said. "At least *I* was. Who knows what you were doing in your class."

"I studied that stuff, too," Iva said, indignant.

"Anyway, I measured my leg with my ruler. From my knee to the top of my foot is exactly twelve inches long." Heaven flexed her leg to demonstrate. "I figured it would come in handy if I wanted to know how long a foot was."

Iva was astonished. Why hadn't *she* ever thought of that? If she wasn't careful, Heaven could turn out to be a better discoverer than her.

"Okay," she said. "Check and see how deep it is."

Heaven stuck her leg in the hole. "Exactly one foot. But I don't see any cannon."

"General Braddock could have been off an inch or two," Iva said. "Keep digging."

Heaven puffed her damp bangs upward and jammed the shovel in partway. *Ching!* went the shovel. "I hit something!"

"Must be the cannon!" Iva stooped so quick she got a stitch in her side. The shovel had revealed a sliver of yellow metal. "Gold! Dig!"

With the shovel, Heaven scraped around the edges. Then she reached down and tugged it free. "It's awful big for a gold coin."

"Money was bigger in those days." Iva felt like she was going to keel over as Heaven pulled out a flat dirt-encrusted object.

"Here's your treasure."

It was a brass plaque that said *Office*.

Iva's hopes dropped to her toenails. A door sign! A stupid door sign!

"Maybe," she said thinly, "we need to dig in a new spot." The handle of the shovel was slapped into her palm. "What's this?"

"Your turn," Heaven said.

"But you're the strong one! That's why you're helping me!" Iva protested.

"I'm hot and tired. And I have blisters on my hands."

"You're my silent partner!" Iva said. "You're not supposed to complain."

Heaven plunked down on a patch of grass. "Let me know when you find the cannon. I'll help you count the money."

Iva jabbed the shovel into the hole. Maybe it was better this way. *She* would discover the treasure first. *She* would get all the credit, which she deserved.

She scooped a shovelful of dirt and threw it over her shoulder. Dirt spattered Heaven's shirt.

"Hey!" Heaven jumped up. "You did that on purpose!"

Iva held the shovel out in front of her like a weapon. "No I didn't! Honest! The shovel slipped."

Heaven grabbed a rotten plum and threw it on Iva's shirt. "Oops! My hand slipped."

"Okay, this is war!" Iva looked around and found a delightfully smelly fish.

As she bent to pick it up, she slid in the muck. She put her hand behind her to support herself but plunged backward into the hole. Her fingers touched something rough . . . and wooden.

"The plug!" she cried. "I found the wooden plug on the cannon!"

Heaven dropped a mushy grapefruit. "What?"

"Help me!" With her hands, she cleared away crumbs of dirt, revealing a round piece of wood.

Heaven kneeled beside her, scrabbling in the hole.

"We should feel the outside of the cannon soon," Iva said, eager to touch cool cast iron.

They scratched and scraped feverishly until sweat streamed off their faces.

Finally Iva quit digging. Her hands and clothes were filthy. She felt like crying. "Where's the iron part of the cannon? There's only a long stick of wood. I don't get it."

"There's only one thing left to do," Heaven said, sitting back on her heels. "Pray."

"What?" Iva blinked at her. "Right now? Pray for *what*?"

"For the treasure." Heaven's grubby hand took Iva's. "Look up at the sky and close your eyes."

"I thought you looked *down* and closed your eyes when you prayed."

"If you want this to work, you have to do it my way." Heaven tilted her head back and shut her eyes. Iva did, too.

Heaven intoned, "Bless this ground, and bless this . . . garbage. Bless this piece of wood we found, and help us find the gold."

"What in the name of Adam's house cat are you kids doing?"

Iva's eyes flew open like window shades.

Swannanoah Priddy towered over them.

"Swan, we discovered something real important," Iva said. "Can you help us dig it up?" She'd have to give Swannanoah part of the gold, but it would be worth it.

"You discovered," Swannanoah said, "a post."

"A post?" Iva repeated weakly.

"Long time ago there used to be a wood fence around the dump. The fence fell down and sunk into the ground." Swannanoah walked away, chuckling.

Iva wondered how long before everyone in town knew Iva and Heaven Honeycutt were found praying over a rotted fence post.

Chapter Eleven

Uncertain Star

The pup tent smelled like the inside of Arden's closet, but Iva didn't care. She was alone, except for Sweetlips.

Uncle Buddy had put her tent up that afternoon. "Have fun camping out," he said before leaving for his shift at the box factory. Iva didn't explain the tent was *not* a place to play.

She sat cross-legged on the quilt she'd brought from her room, along with some of her earthly possessions. She opened her crayon box. Her hand hovered over the bottom row, where her best crayons lived. Her favorite crayon, Blue Green, was missing from the number one spot.

Reminding herself to tie Arden's socks into knots, she chose her second favorite, Teal Blue. She leaned over her old third-grade map and drew a five-pointed star in the middle of Virginia to mark Uncertain. Well, where she *thought* Uncertain was.

She stared at the star until it seemed to drift into North Carolina. She was supposed to have been the star of Uncertain this summer. But she was such a rotten discoverer, she didn't even know the location of her own town.

Iva ripped her map in two. The pieces fluttered onto the October 1939 issue of *National Geographic*. She had planned to read an article called "We Keep House on an Active Volcano," but now she didn't feel like it.

Ludwell Honeycutt's tire-pressure book lay next to the magazine. Iva picked it up and opened to the first page. *The Book of Great Discoveries Made by Iva Honeysuckle*. What great discoveries? She hadn't found Braddock's gold. Her great discovery summer was a total flop. She hadn't gotten her picture in *The Uncertain Star*. And . . . she had let her great-grandfather down.

"In here! Hurry!"

Lily Pearl shoved through the tent flap. Howard scuttled in behind her with Lily Pearl's Halloween trick-or-treat pail.

"What are you brats doing?" Iva said, crowded against Sweetlips.

"We had *pork chops* for supper," Lily Pearl said, as if she'd endured a hideous crime. "Time and again I told Mama how much I hate pork chops, but she *will not listen*. So I'm leaving home."

"What about you?" Iva asked Howard. "You *like* pork chops."

"He goes where I go," Lily Pearl stated. She took the pumpkin pail and unpacked five men's handkerchiefs, her mother's rhinestone bracelet, and one Blue Green crayon.

Iva pounced on it. "*You* stole my crayon! And what're you doing with Daddy's handkerchiefs?"

"They pack nice," Lily Pearl said. "We can hide in here, can't we?"

"No. Howard, get off my *National Geographic* magazine. It's very old."

Outside, something screeched, like two cats fighting on a back fence.

"*Found a peanut, found a peanut, found a peanut just now. Just now I found a peanut, found a peanut just now.*"

The tent flap flipped back. Arden and Hunter poked their heads in, singing, "*It was rotten, it was rotten, it was rot-ten just now. Just now it was rotten, it was rot-ten just now.*"

"Go *away!*" Iva exclaimed.

"We're joining your little campout," Arden said. "We even brought marshmallows."

"Take them back," Iva said. "You're not invited."

"Will you tell ghost stories?" Lily Pearl asked. "Howard and me love to be scared."

"*Ate it anyway, ate it anyway, ate it a-nyway just*

now. *Just now I ate it anyway, ate it a-nyway just now.*"

"Shut up that stupid song!" Iva said, pushing Arden's face.

Arden slapped Iva's hand away. "It's a camp-out song."

"And we sing it real good," said Hunter.

"*Got a stomachache, got a stomachache, got a sto-machache just now. Just now I got a stomachache, got a sto-machache just now.*"

Iva had a stomachache listening to them. "Get *out* just now!"

"You should be glad Mama even let you camp out," Arden said. "You left Daddy's tools all over town. Cazy Sparkle found them and sold them at her yard sale. Mama had to buy back our own tools."

"I spent the whole day cleaning the shed," Iva said. "My punishment is over."

But it wasn't.

Arden and Hunter continued to sing. "*Called the doctor, called the doctor, called the doc-tor just now. Just now I called the doctor, called the doc-tor just now.*"

"If you don't get out, you're going to need a doctor!" Iva felt like running away herself. Why couldn't she have five minutes' peace?

"I want a marshmallow," Howard said.

Arden stopped caterwauling. "Hunt, you know that girl in our class, Burgin Clatterbuck? Her mother *makes* marshmallows from scratch. She uses Knox gelatin."

Hunter wrinkled her nose. "Ewww." Then she joined Arden in the next chorus.

"Died anyway, died anyway—"

Iva stuffed the handkerchiefs and rhinestone bracelet back in Lily Pearl's pumpkin pail, and thrust it at her. "Get out, everybody. Right *now!*"

Arden and Hunter backed out, laughing. Lily Pearl crawled out in a huff, Howard crabbing behind her.

"I'm never running away to *your* house again," Lily Pearl flung at Iva.

"Me neither!" Howard ran to catch up to Lily Pearl.

"Why wasn't I born an only child?" Iva said to Sweetlips.

He put his nose down on his front paws and sighed. He didn't know, either.

Iva lay down on the quilt and watched fireflies flickering in the grape arbor. Lily Pearl and Howard played Witchy, May I, leaping from shadow to shadow. Arden's and Hunter's faint voices sang, *"Went to heaven, went to heaven, went to hea-ven just now. Just now I went to heaven, went to hea-ven just now."*

The cousins were paired off, having fun, living up to Iva's mother and Aunt Sissy Two's grand plan. All but Iva.

Iva felt at rock bottom. Nothing worse could happen.

Then she heard something snuffling outside the tent.

"Iva? Can I come in?"

Iva closed her eyes. If she pretended to be dead, Heaven would go away.

"I've got something for you." Heaven's voice rose in a tantalizing lilt.

Iva smacked the tent flap open. "What?"

Heaven steamrollered herself inside the tent, carrying her pillow under her arm.

"Don't get comfortable," Iva said. "You're not staying." Heaven seemed to take up more room than Arden, Lily Pearl, Howard, and Hunter all together.

Heaven dug something out from her pillowcase. "I just came back from Cazy Sparkle's yard sale. I put that TV lamp on layaway and got you this."

In the faint light, Iva could make out a skimpy-haired doll in a dusty ruffled skirt. "Thank you, but I don't play with dolls."

"It's not a doll." Heaven turned it upside down. "See, you hide your extra roll of toilet paper under the skirt."

"In case you haven't noticed, my tent doesn't have a bathroom."

"Put *other* things inside it," Heaven said, sliding out a shiny brass sign that said *Office*. "I cleaned it up for you. Since you're into that discovering stuff, I thought you'd like this."

She *did* like the sign. And the fact that Heaven finally admitted Iva had a real life's ambition. "Thanks. I'll put it on my bedroom door." Not that it would keep anybody out.

"You won't mind if I take the doll back?"

"No." Some things never changed.

"I have something else for you," Heaven said. "Close your eyes and open your mouth."

"The last time I did that, I kicked the bottom of my cradle out—"

"Iva, just do it!"

Iva closed her eyes and opened her mouth. Something cool and sweet dropped on her tongue. Butter rum!

"Hey, that's the kind of Life Saver Ludwell gave Daddy when he was a little boy," she said.

"My daddy, too," Heaven said. "My daddy is younger than Uncle Sonny, but he still remembers our great-grandfather. He's told me a few things about him."

"You didn't come to bring me a toilet paper doll you took back and a Life Saver." Iva knew Heaven always had an ulterior motive. "What do you want?"

"Can I sleep over?" Heaven asked. "We never do that. Hunter sleeps over with Arden all the time."

"I know," Iva said. "I feel like I have three sisters most of the time."

"Well, can I?"

They laid down their heads outside the tent. Iva thought about Yard Sale, the world's cutest kitten that Heaven was allowed to keep at Miz Compton's house. She thought about Heaven's job as assistant church-school teacher. She thought about how Heaven hadn't gotten into trouble for digging in the dump yesterday—well, for leaving tools all over town. Heaven, it seemed, had everything on earth. Why should Iva let her stay over?

Yet . . . there was something comforting about her sturdy self lying next to Iva.

"You're taking an awful long time," Heaven said. "I guess that means no."

"No. You can stay."

"Thanks." Heaven lay on her side, facing Iva, and huffed in her ear, "Yesterday was fun, wasn't it?"

"Digging garbage in the hot sun is your idea of fun?"

"Yeah."

Iva giggled. It *had* been kind of fun, in a weird way. Even more weird, she and Heaven had actually gotten along.

"You know, you do interesting stuff," Heaven said. "Like that treasure map. You figured out the clues and looked for it all by yourself. And you almost found it!"

"The gold could be anywhere. *If* it's there at all," Iva said glumly.

"I bet you'll find it." Iva knew Heaven was

tuning up for an all-night gab fest. "I could help you look. We could—"

"I want to go to sleep now." If she didn't cut her off, Heaven would jabber until daybreak.

"Okay. G'night." And, miracle of miracles, her cousin shut up.

Heaven conked out almost instantly. Iva worried the tent would collapse under the force of her snoring.

Rolling over, Iva gazed up at the sky. Katydids *wheek-wheeked* in the treetops. A thin moon seemed to curve around the first stars.

She wondered if all the stars had been discovered yet. She wondered about that friend business. Miz Compton could be right. If Iva wanted a friend, maybe she'd have to be one first.

Heaven mumbled something. Great, Iva thought. She talks in her sleep.

A white streak arced across the sky. Iva traced the path of the falling star, fascinated. It seemed

certain where it was going. The star appeared to drop behind Heaven's head.

Was that a sign? Was the friend she'd been looking for really her mouth-breathing, trouble-some double-first cousin?

The tent flap fluttered as Heaven snored.

Maybe, Iva thought. Maybe the grand plan might work after all.